DEATH WITNESSED

A Poison Ink Mystery

BETH BYERS

SUMMARY

March 1937

Georgette Dorothy Marsh published a book when she was no longer able to afford cream for her tea. Without enough imagination to tell a story on her own, she wrote about her neighbors instead. Only her book became a best seller and her village was ready to take up arms.

She never expected the money let alone the results. One man died just after publication. After a pot of lapsang souchong at the local tea room, Miss Marsh witnesses another murder. When Miss Marsh realizes this murder is connected to her book as well, she turns to her friend Mr. Aaron. Once again, he brings along his nephew and they are back to attempting to find the killer, ensuring that Miss Marsh isn't the next victim, and hiding the real person behind this poisoned book.

For Taryn.
It's a special friend that you can trust to be your very first reader.
You were perfect then and even better now.
Thanks babe.
XOXO

And for awkward, twenty-three year old Amanda
The fodder for this story is delightfully funny these days.
Who knew?

I

GEORGETTE DOROTHY MARSH

If there was a goddess looking down on Bard's Crook on that sunny spring day, it was that minx Atë—the goddess of pranks and mischief. She'd cast her wily eye on the village, took in the new widow, Harriet Lawrence, happily sipping tea in her parlor while she curled up on her chaise lounge with a plate of biscuits. Was it Atë or fate that had Harriet glance out the window, note the sun rays pouring down on the wood and decide to venture into those depths?

If it was Atë, perhaps she also cast her sly gaze on the doctor's wife watching her rambunctious lads chase through the garden. If any creature would love those filthy bright-eyed creatures, it was their mother, seconded only by Atë.

Perhaps then the goddess shifted her gaze from the boys to their mother's friend, Virginia Baker. Mrs. Virginia Baker was a woman that Atë loved to hate. Virginia was not as beautiful as she made it seem nor was she as clever as she portrayed herself to be. It was rare for someone to consider again on the things Virginia had previously said with confidence and a little something in her air. If, perhaps, her words were weighted against facts, all would be shocked to realize how often Virginia's thumb had been on the proverbial scale.

There was one person who wouldn't be shocked in the slightest. It was to her that Atë would next turn her gaze, leaving behind Virginia Baker for Atë's favorite villager. Like all those who were roguish, Atë enjoyed the dichotomy presented by Georgette Dorothy Marsh. When one looked upon Miss Marsh, the discovery was an artless old maid. Well into her twenties with her looks as unpresuming as her artless demeanor, she was nothing that required a second glance. With her common, medium brown hair, medium brown eyes, far too many freckles, lips that were neither thin nor full, she was—to put it plainly—unremarkable. When one was to add in her tendency to watch the world around her and rarely comment with her true thoughts, it was a rare individual indeed who knew her for what she was.

To know Georgette Dorothy Marsh, one had to journey behind her facade, behind her soft voice, behind her quiet demeanor, and peek into those candid eyes. Once one saw how cleverly she took in the world, the obliviousness of her neighbors was perhaps more shocking than anything else.

Her reputation, indeed the very way she was treated, was even more shocking given that Georgette had recently started styling her hair to accent her rather delicate features and was wearing both clothes that fit as well as clothes that were not threadbare and worn when they were given to her.

It seemed that entrenched notions, especially these that had existed for decades, were, in fact, impossible to adjust.

That morning, Georgette Dorothy Marsh walked out of her cottage door rather innocently. Was she the secret author, Joseph Jones? Georgie wouldn't admit to it when she could sidestep the question with an inane comment. She'd tuck back her wispy hair, avert her solemn gaze, and hope her pale skin didn't prove her a liar.

On that day, Dorcas, Bea, and Susan cavorted at her feet. The puppies she'd rescued from a box on the creek had turned into chubby dogs. They had those precious, loving gazes that only dogs possessed, proclaiming their love with each soulful glance. Being utterly adored, even if it was just by dogs, was the missing piece of Georgette's life. She grinned at her thought and was grateful that no one could read her mind. Utter adoration was all that she was missing? What cheek!

Well, adoration and more tea. Her most recent glorious splurge had been on a Bombay chai tea. She and her maid, Eunice, brewed the tea in milk, and it was a glorious treat. She was considering a blend of teas with coconut, roses, and green teas as well as a fruit tea made of golden pear. Then there was that cagey magician who had created a mixture of black tea, coffee, cocoa, and spices. Georgette's next order would certainly include some of that black magic.

"I read it again," Marian called as she joined Georgie with her own dog. "I just love it so much."

Georgie gave Marian a quelling look and ordered, "Don't speak of it."

Marian just laughed merrily. "I can't help it. Now that I know who it is behind those characters, I just enjoy it all the more. Did Mrs. Baker really throw herself at one of Miss Hallowton's boarders?"

Georgette sighed and said low, "He did have an auto." She suddenly cleared her throat as the woman approached.

"Speak of the devil." Marian tucked her arm through Georgette's. "She's become rather interested in me since my cousin, Harrison, visited."

"He also has an auto," Georgie whispered wickedly, hiding her mischievous humor behind a vague expression. "Something avaricious this way comes."

Marian bit back a laugh and then used the humor in her voice to call a merry, "Hullo there! Lovely day for a walk."

"Marian!" Mrs. Baker said. "How lovely to see you."

Virginia Baker was a curvaceous and stylish woman who presented herself as the belle of every ball. It took a clever eye to notice the too-small eyes and thin lips behind Mrs. Baker's occasionally engaging manner and perfect grooming.

Marian squeezed Georgette's arm at the snub.

"Good morning, Mrs. Baker," Georgette said. "It is indeed lovely to run across friendly faces on our little ramble."

Georgette smiled politely as Mrs. Baker's gaze shot to her, narrowed, and then returned to Marian with that charming grin. Georgette had thought, more than once, that if a King Cobra had a smile, it would be rather like Virginia Baker's.

"Dear Marian, I was looking for you. I'm having a little gathering at my house to enjoy this weather. Just a few friends, conversation, tea and cakes, you know. It would be lovely if you and your cousin, Harrison, would come."

Marian glanced between Virginia and Georgette, clearly

rather startled to personally witness the scorn. Georgette's expression was a sort of half-absent blankness that Marian had already realized missed nothing.

Georgette could see Marian's fury, but in her opinion, this was a gift straight from the gods. Her book had been missing these little moments to give it flavor, and this one would do so well for her newest character. Mr. Aaron wanted the next book even more quickly than the last, and this would do quite well for the one she was just finishing.

The click-clack of the keys on her typewriter over the last few weeks had been simply too exhilarating. She was thankful that no one could hear it beyond her cottage. She'd verified that with both Marian and her maid, Eunice.

Her first book was something of an inexplicable success. She had rather innocently based her book off of her neighbors. She'd assumed they'd never know and hadn't worried that she had been a bit unkind. Who would imagine that the book would sell as hers had? No one, she told herself every time she felt guilty about her neighbors' reactions. They despised it. Which would have been hard enough to bear, but it had also caused a murder. A murder! Even now, she was shocked to realize that such a thing had happened.

Perhaps she should feel guilty, but she couldn't quite reach enduring remorse. Georgie had not lifted the cricket bat, but she had witnessed the dawning happiness in the widow's gaze. She neither took credit for the happiness nor the murder and counted herself blessed that no one had realized who had written the book.

"Just a few friends—" Virginia repeated as though it somehow excused not inviting Georgette.

"Oh look," Georgette said vaguely. They'd reached the library and there was a sign in the window. She stepped away from the other two, glancing back and seeing only Marian's gaze. Georgette dared a wicked wink and then pretended to be absorbed by the little posting.

After she read it the first time, she read it again.

ALL WELCOME
WEEKLY WRITERS GROUP
TUESDAYS 7:00 P.M., SHARP
SIGN UP SHEET INSIDE

Georgette was concerned with her lack of inventiveness in her books. The one that would be coming out soon only had one character that was entirely fictional. Perhaps she could learn something from other aspiring writers. Her head tilted as she considered. Yes, she would certainly attend. She walked inside to speak to the librarian, another old maid from Bard's Crook.

Miss Hallowton was standing near the checkout desk. Her face was fierce as she tersely asked, "If you're here to ask for The Further Adventures of Harper's Bend, the wait list is at capacity."

Georgette's eyes widened, and she shook her head quickly before Miss Hallowton could read anything else in her reaction. "I would like to sign up for the writing group," she said quietly.

If anything Miss Hallowton's scowl deepened. "This is for a serious pursuit of writing."

Georgette nibbled her bottom lip. "I would still like to sign up. Are there rules that say I cannot?"

Miss Hallowton pulled the clipboard out and smacked it down on the counter. "You'll be asked to leave if you're late or do not do your assignments."

Georgette simply nodded.

"You'll be expected to take turns providing refreshments. I will not be the only one to do so."

Georgette nodded again. Miss Hallowton turned to the portion of the library that was the post office and handed Georgette a few letters and two rather telling parcels. One was of three books that had been kindly sent, she had been promised, with false book covers. The other was her newest tea acquisition. With the publication of her newest book, Georgette had rewarded herself with pure luxuries. A box of Belgian chocolates, a rather extensive sampling of tea blends from a new shop, and a delightful Chinese style teapot made with purple clay called zisha.

As Georgette thanked Miss Hallowton, the woman asked again. "Are you certain you want to join the writers group?"

Georgette nodded. Miss Hallowton huffed and wrote down: Miss Georgette Marsh. Who, Georgette thought, was quite capable of hearing the librarian's low muttering as she put the clipboard away. "I suppose we'll have to take turns getting inane feedback until she gets bored."

Georgette's solemn expression didn't fade despite Miss Hallowton's mood. Georgette did feel that Miss Hallowton, who was quite clever, would be significantly lovelier if she were just the smallest bit cheerier. Once again, Georgette reminded herself that she did not know the details of Miss Hallowton's circumstances. It was possible, however, to extrapolate that like so many, she was struggling to get by. The woman ran both the post office and the library as well as keeping boarders. That much working alone told Georgette enough.

She did want to be part of this writers group if it helped

ensure her third book was as good as it could be. It seemed improbable that success somehow was more stressful than not having enough money to survive the winter, but it seemed that it was.

"I would be happy to bring the refreshments for the first meeting," Georgette offered consolingly. "Just let me know how many to account for, and I'll come a bit early with something or other."

Miss Hallowton was mildly appeased as Georgette's friend, Marian, opened the door to the library.

"Miss Marsh?" Marian called from the doorway to the library. "Did you get what you needed?"

Georgette turned to Marian and nodded quietly, and the girl came the rest of the way into the room. She wasn't a girl, not really, but so often Georgette felt that her youth combined with her utter lack of worries made her seem unfairly young.

With a hidden, wicked grin, Georgette told Marian, "The wait list for that book you wanted is full."

Marian's startled gaze flicked between Georgette and Miss Hallowton before she realized the book. "The Further Adventures of Harper's Bend?"

Georgette nodded. Marian laughed too hard for such a casual thing and earned a hard glare from Georgette. "Oh, I ordered a copy. I am hoping that it will be delivered early."

"I doubt that will happen," Miss Hallowton said sourly. "I can't get early copies here at the library, so why should you? Everyone wants that book after what happened with the last one. The more I think about it, the more certain I am that it was all a bunch of odd coincidences."

"That's just what Miss Marsh says," Marian replied, ignoring Georgette's veiled glare.

"Mmmph," was Miss Hallowton's only reply. She finally eyed Marian. "Unless you're here to check out a book, work on something quietly, or sign up for the writing class as Miss Marsh has done, you'd be welcomed to loiter elsewhere."

Georgette turned immediately as she was already concerned they'd left the dogs too long, but she didn't quite escape in time to avoid Marian's exclamation. "A writers group?"

"Yes," Miss Hallowton nearly growled. "I hardly have time for dilettantes. Some of us are pursuing a serious writing career."

Marian bit down on her bottom lip hard as she snorted. "Oh, do sign me up. I have been scribbling my own stories lately with the help of a friend. She is already a published writer. Quite excellent, in fact. Something of a surprise bestseller."

Georgette's gaze narrowed, but she could do nothing more than escape the library before Marian's barbs and lies revealed Georgette's nature as the iniquitous Joseph Jones.

2

CHARLES AARON

"I'm confused," Joseph said, leaning back to puff on his cigar while the waiter cleared his plate away.

"What is all that hard to understand?" Charles asked, giving his nephew a fierce look to change the subject. "I took Miss Harriet Moore to dinner and a play. It's hardly notable."

"Oh, of course." Joseph Aaron chuckled heartily, almost choking on his cigar smoke.

Charles slowly lit his pipe, preferring the sweeter scent of pipe tobacco, before he leaned back himself, lifting his glass of port with his free hand. He knew, of course, exactly why Joseph was laughing, but Charles wasn't a masochist and preferred not to linger on his agony.

"Tell me about Miss Moore," Joseph said, with the corners of his mouth still quivering.

"She is a sweet woman. Kind. Ah—"

Joseph already looked as bored as Charles had been that evening. The more he thought of not being a bachelor, the more he told himself that he should very much dislike married life. When the thought wouldn't leave him be, he decided to let his gaze roam the field, so to speak. To say that Harriet Moore was better suited for another man was, perhaps, the kindest way to describe the evening.

"You were bored dumb, were you not?" Joseph asked his uncle.

"Why would you say that?" Charles kept the question light as though his nephew could not possibly be correct, but his tone didn't succeed.

"Does Miss Moore write books?"

Charles sniffed and then sipped from his port.

"Is she quietly witty?"

Charles didn't bother to answer that question in favor of sipping from his port once again.

"I know that I'm younger than you," Joseph told Charles seriously. "To be honest, I invited you to dinner for your advice. However—" Joseph searched Charles's face almost fervently as if he wanted to mentally press what he was about to say into Charles. His uncle lifted a brow and Joseph continued. "However, you're in love with Miss Marsh."

Charles laughed, but even to his ear, it was hollow.

"If you'd known when you read that book that it was more than a clever tale, you'd have been half-entranced with that alone," Joseph said. "Having met the people in her town, having seen how they treat her, having seen her kindness and her...her...fortitude, you fell head over heels, and all you're doing with Miss Moore and her ilk is stalling."

"Cheeky," Charles said, setting his port down. He knew

his face was emotionless, but he was reeling at the sheer, blunt honesty and the way the idea resounded in his mind. Just hearing her name was enough to make him wonder what she was doing. He'd told himself for a while now that he was only wondering because he wanted that next book, but Charles knew that he was lying to himself when faced with Joseph's clever eye.

"May I ask you a serious question?" Joseph's gaze flicked to between his cigar and Charles's face without ever meeting Charles's gaze. Joseph's face turned red on his cheeks and his ears, and Charles lifted a brow.

"Of course," Charles said.

"I—" Joseph cleared his throat and then said, "I am, perhaps, a little, well…"

Charles lifted a brow. "Does this question of yours have anything to do with the lovely Miss Marian Parker?"

Joseph cleared his throat and admitted, "I find that my occasional forays into Bard's Crook aren't quite enough to satisfy my desire to see her, but I am also a bit—well, I'm not quite sure that I love her."

"Yet you're so very sure that I have those feelings for Miss Marsh?"

"If God himself crafted you a mate, I'm not sure the match would be better for you than Miss Marsh, Uncle."

Charles snorted at that and Joseph shook his head.

"Let's try again to lay it out in a different way, dear uncle."

Charles wasn't able to hide his irritation, but Joseph only grinned. This is what happened from not being all that much older than his nephew. Charles's other nephew, Robert, was barely hanging onto any shreds of respect for him either, and only because he worked for Charles's company.

"By all means," Charles said sarcastically, "proceed."

"Miss Moore was boring."

"What does that have to do with my feelings for another?"

"That woman you were seeing when Robert and I were at university," Joseph added. "You told us you could not imagine a lifetime of such inane chatter."

"Again—" Charles started, but Joseph held up a hand.

"Miss Thornton," Joseph added. "You said she hadn't read a book for pleasure in her lifetime."

Charles sniffed and took a puff off his cigar.

"Miss Vance, she had an unkind twist to her mouth."

Charles chuckled at that one. He had said that regarding the woman, and it was true as well.

"The one with the most luxurious brown eyes and hair. She was an English Cleopatra and wickedly clever. Do you remember the excuse for that one?"

Charles did, in fact, remember and was choosing not to repeat it.

Joseph had no such compunction. "Too beautiful and likely to turn to fat. There is literally no pleasing you."

Charles puffed his cigar again. He didn't think being a bit—ah—selective about the woman sharing your bed, life, and children was wrong. He was considering the rest of his life.

"You realize," Joseph said idly, "sooner or later those fellows in Bard's Crook are going to wake up to what's in their midst."

Charles was not about to be pushed about by threats from

his nephew. If Miss Marsh found companionship and love, he wished her the best. The thought of it was not causing his heart to freeze in his chest or his back teeth to ache.

"Back to your question," Charles snapped.

"How do I get to know her better without leading her on?"

"You're due for some time off," Charles told him. "We both are, to be honest, though I don't know any businessman who truly leaves his business behind." He could say the same of his nephew's career in law enforcement.

"It is an idyllic town," Joseph said, leaning back. "Perhaps just what is needed to clear my palette from London after the last round of cases."

"I'm sure you need to cleanse your palette from that string of robberies."

"The things," Joseph said with a wide, cheery grin, "that mankind do to one another. It could make one quite soul sick."

"Indeed," Charles replied dryly.

"You'll be coming," Joseph said.

"Why would I do that?"

"To remind yourself of what you're talking yourself out of. I won't interfere, I swear it on my honor. We both need clarity. Bard's Crook is a quiet little village. What could happen?"

❦

GEORGETTE DOROTHY MARSH

"Miss Georgie," Eunice said from the doorway of the

second bedroom that had become Georgie's office. "Miss Hallowton is at the door."

Georgette looked up from her manuscript. It was done, she thought. Her stomach ached at the idea of sending it off too early. Though Mr. Aaron had been so kind about her last book, she wasn't quite sure he liked it as much as he said he did. He'd sworn he'd love it before he even read it. He'd published it, but maybe with the assumption that the people who loved the first would enjoy the second? Perhaps he didn't like the second book, but it still made good business sense to publish it?

If so, she couldn't count on that continuing with subsequent books. It was one thing to let the public decide for one book, but if they decided against—oh! She wanted desperately to read the reviews to see what people were saying and decide whether her worries were only unruly nerves or were legitimate concerns.

Her fingers slid over the pages of the second book. Marian had taken one of the copies home with her the previous day, but Georgette knew better than to trust her friend's reviews. Perhaps if Eunice bothered to read it. The woman had known Georgette since her babyhood. Having changed Georgette's nappies prevented the woman from feeling the slightest obligation to coddle Georgette's sensibilities.

If she were being entirely honest with herself, she quite liked this one more than the last two combined. The characters had grown and changed and even though the idea of what they might do was based upon her neighbors, even still, the situations were entirely fictional.

"Miss Georgie?" Eunice said again, opening the door wider. "Did you want me to tell her that you're indisposed?"

Georgette pushed up from her desk. "No, of course not. I'm afraid I'm rather lost in my thoughts, Eunice."

"The book will be fine."

Georgette smiled gently, kissing the woman on the cheek. "Thank you for thinking so."

"Miss Parker was giggling over that second book before she made it out the door."

"She wants to like it," Georgette said, simply. "She'll look for the good in it and ignore the rest."

"It's a good book, Miss Georgie. I read both of them, you know. They weren't half bad."

Georgette grinned at that half compliment and walked down the steep, narrow steps of her cottage. Her parents had inherited it from an aunt, and it was full of character and inexplicable squeaks.

"Oh hello, Miss Hallowton," Georgette said quietly. "So nice of you to stop by."

"You look flushed. Were you napping?" Miss Hallowton glanced about the cottage, her gaze lingering on the newer furniture for a moment before Georgette invited her to sit.

"Just working on some things upstairs," Georgette said vaguely. "May I offer you a cuppa?"

Before Miss Hallowton could decline or accept, Eunice carried in a tea tray.

"Oh, thank you," Georgette said. "I have been wanting a cup and have been too distracted to ask. Miss Hallowton?"

The woman accepted and Georgette poured her a cup, adding only lemon. Georgette left plenty of room for cream in hers and rather too much sugar before she sipped. Eunice, the clever woman, had brought in a decent Earl Grey tea. A rather nice blend but none of Georgette's recent splurges.

"You'll run to fat if you keep drinking your tea like a child."

"I suppose I might," Georgie said. She had, in fact, gained some weight since her finances had turned, but she attributed the change to being able to afford more than eggs, sardines, and soup. She'd been forced to let out her new skirt and considered upon the issue before she'd decided that not being bone-thin was a blessing. She intended to give the extra flesh as much concern as whatever was happening in the wilds of Mongolia.

Miss Hallowton sniffed and then pulled a sheet of paper from her satchel. "This is a list of those who intend to come to our writing group. I'll have the pot ready, but I'll expect you to provide tea and coffee. Perhaps something to nibble upon. We'll be meeting from 7:00 p.m. to 8:30. Bring writing you're prepared to share. Will you have that ready by then?"

"I will." In fact, Georgette had about four stories that were all begun with imagination alone. One, in fact, was nearly finished as far as the conclusion being written. She was not, however, prepared to share it with Mr. Aaron. What if she hadn't succeeded? Why was it that she was more nervous now than she'd been with that first book?

"See that you do," Miss Hallowton said, setting aside her mostly full cup of tea and standing. "We can't all nap the day away. There is much to do before bed for one such as I."

"Have a lovely evening," Georgette replied, following Miss Hallowton to the door and seeing her out.

"What a sour old thing," Eunice said. "As if you haven't struggled as hard as she. She's lucky you are as kind as you are. Your second and third bedrooms are quite a bit better than what she's offering those boarders of hers, and you wouldn't water the soup as she does. She little realizes that you chose not to open your door to boarders because she needed them."

"It turned out for the best, dear Eunice. We would have hated having boarders, and I rather enjoy writing."

"Those dark circles under your eyes say otherwise," Eunice said, her gaze passing over Georgette and finding her wanting. "You need to sleep more and write less. As if I don't hear you groan when you stand. It's not a good thing to write until your hips and back hurt."

Georgette smiled. "Perhaps you're right."

3

GEORGETTE DOROTHY MARSH

"You'll never guess," Marian said as she burst through the kitchen door a week later. She had a book under her arm and a basket with the post in it. Georgette guessed by the parcel from the tea vendor that her own post was included.

"You got my post," Georgette said, waving Marian to the kitchen table where she had been lingering over her tea. She had finished polishing her book and had sat down at the table to sip her tea, munch her toast, and write a note to Mr. Aaron to go with the manuscript.

"Well yes," Marian said, thrusting the basket at Georgette. "I was chatting with Miss Hallowton. She cross-examined me about my writing piece. I'm terrified to show it to her."

"It's good," Georgette assured her.

"It's not clever like yours, but that's beside the point,"

Marian gushed. "She was telling me that she had one of her rooms taken by two Londoners who needed a break from city life but needed to be close enough to engage in their business if necessary."

Georgette didn't glance up at that. If Marian kept speaking, Georgette didn't hear it. Her attention was entirely claimed by an envelope from Mr. Aaron's office. She'd received one of these before, and she knew she'd be reading reviews.

She wiped her butter knife clean with her napkin and opened the envelope with shaking fingers, whispering to herself that everyone was not going to be pleased. A note came out first with a simple:

> *Miss Marsh,*
> *You are to be congratulated on such a release.*
> *C. Aaron*

Georgette let out a shaky breath and opened the first review. *Even more charming than the last.* She closed her eyes in utter relief and then looked up with actual tears in her eyes. "I'm crying over my reviews."

"I told you it was wonderful," Marian said. "Did you hear what I said?"

"You would have liked it if it was terrible." Georgette dared to look at the next clipping. *Trite, but pleasing enough for the easily pleased.*

She grinned at that one. Pleasing enough for her as well. She glanced at the next one. *Joseph Jones was remarkable in his debut. The surer hand of the writer was all that was needed to have this reader already begging for the next.*

"Did you hear what I said?" Marian asked.

Georgette glanced up blankly.

"Are you listening this time?"

Georgette blinked. Eunice snorted and Georgette looked at her instead. Her normally staid gaze was bright with something. Humor? Was it at Georgette's expense? What had she missed?

"What happened?" Georgette asked, actually listening.

"Miss Hallowton has new boarders."

"She always has boarders," Georgette replied, sipping her tea. Good reviews surely justified this latest indulgence. At first she wasn't sure if she liked it, as the combination of coffee, tea, and cocoa bean was somehow very wrong. Once Georgette moved past what she expected, however, she discovered utter delight.

"She has Londoners as boarders."

"Well, I suppose if they can't go all the way to the seaside and just need fresh air, Bard's Crook has it in abundance. Lovely rambles. A decent pub. One could do worse."

Marian spoke in her impersonation of Miss Hallowton's prim voice. "That detective from London and his uncle of all people."

Georgette blinked rapidly, trying to understand what she was saying. "I'm confused."

"You aren't confused, love," Eunice told her. "You're uncertain. It's an interesting development."

"Why?" Marian demanded.

"If they're here for the air, I'll eat my soap." Eunice glanced between the two women and then shook her head even more dramatically. "They're here for you two."

Marian's gaze widened and a blush grew from her cheeks and down her neck. Georgette grinned at the girl.

"You're delightful, darling. Of course, Detective Aaron wanted to see you again. Who wouldn't?"

"And Mr. Aaron?" Marian demanded.

Georgette stared and then glanced at Eunice before shaking her head.

"Yes," Marian said as Georgette shook her head again.

"Of course not."

"Yes," Marian and Eunice both said.

"You're very wrong," Georgette replied. "I'm sure, for Mr. Aaron, it's just what he said. He needed time away from the London air. Perhaps he has too many manuscripts to read and needs time away from the office as well."

"No," Marian told Georgette. "No."

"Marian," Georgette told her gently, "of course, I'm right. Mr. Aaron is a city man with a successful business who, I'm sure, doesn't want for company. I'm only one of his writers—and not even close to the most talented."

"No," Marian said again. "He's here for you."

"You're wrong," Georgette said, laughing them both off and returning to her reviews with a scoffed, "Me!"

***

GEORGETTE LEFT BEHIND CRYING DOGS AS SHE EXITED the cottage with her basket and her satchel. She'd purchased herself the type of leather university bag that the lads carried. It had a long strap that she could use to carry it across her body and would hold not only the book she was reading, but the manuscript she was working on. It was, in fact, once used by Jasper Thornton before he was sent down from Oxford and not allowed to return. She'd leapt at the chance for a pristine leather satchel and had bought it without a second thought.

It was only after she'd turned over the funds to the young man that she'd paused to realize how wonderful it was to be able to buy it without thinking. She had been secretly quite emotional about it. That evening it carried the sample of her writing that she'd spent the afternoon transcribing from her typed story to the hand-written one.

She was, if she were honest with herself, quite nervous. The basket had the coffee beans that Eunice had ground and tea leaves, along with shortbread biscuits and sandwiches. Eunice had made scones and included clotted cream and jam. That, Georgette had told her maid as Eunice packed the basket, had been her pride talking.

Her maid had not disagreed, but Georgette loved a good scone, so she kept her teasing to a minimum.

"There you are," Marian said, closing the garden gate to her great-aunt's cottage behind her. "Harrison is coming, but he's gone ahead because he's quite nervous. I had no idea that he was an aspiring writer. He has written five—five!—novels and hasn't dared to send even one off to a publisher to see what they say. I wasn't supposed to tell anyone that," Marian said with a shrug. "I'm quite jealous he's gotten so far, even if they're awful, but he says he writes to free himself from his work."

"I shall endeavor to be surprised."

"I have little doubt of your capacity," Marian said, hooking her arm through Georgette's. "Every single person who knows you except for, perhaps, four solitary humans, has no idea what you're like. You are, I think, the most accomplished actress I've ever seen."

"Many people have a more public persona," Georgette

told Marian quietly. "That doesn't mean that I'm something odd."

"Georgie!" Marian exclaimed, "I don't think you're odd. I'm in awe."

Georgette shot Marian a quelling look and then followed with, "You are simply inclined to appreciate my quirks."

Marian laughed and then asked, "What are you calling the next book? The Further Further Adventures? The Extended Adventures?"

"The Secrets of Harper's Bend."

Marian rubbed her hands together, hopping on her toes as they walked. "What do I have to do to read it? I'll bake you something delicious. I'll plant bulbs in your garden. I'll —I don't know. What do you want?"

"I'm not ready yet."

Marian sighed. "When you're ready then. Is that Mrs. Baker?" Marian asked in horror as they turned onto the street with the library. "It is! Oh!"

Georgette's mouth twisted, and she realized what she was seeing as she said, "Oh, of course, the signup sheet."

"What do you mean?"

"Your cousin revealed himself and Mrs. Baker saw an opportunity to access him."

"She's at least a decade older than him!"

A bout of laughter burst from Georgette. "Avarice cares less for age than innocence, my love."

CHARLES AARON

"There she is," Joseph said.

Charles followed Joseph's gaze and saw it was on Marian Parker. Next to her was the slender figure of Georgette Marsh. She was laughing, revealing a rare glimpse of just how lovely she was. It was unusual, he realized, to see her laughing.

"Should we go over there?" Joseph asked.

Charles shot his nephew a look. "Supposedly we're in love."

Joseph growled in his throat and then huffed. "Supposedly we're full grown men who aren't afraid to greet friends who are passing by."

Neither of them moved. Finally, Charles stepped onto the street, and Joseph followed. Marian saw them first, but Charles wasn't surprised to see Georgette's gaze fixed farther down the road. An auto had parked near the library, and a rather tall, broad man was getting out of the vehicle.

Georgette said something to Marian, who glanced down the road and waved. She turned Joseph's way a moment later, those honey brown eyes fixated on him. She gave him the quietest smile and started to step towards him, but he held up a hand and crossed with Charles.

It was awkward only for a moment until Georgette, in her sweet, low voice said, "Mr. Aaron! Detective Aaron! What a surprise."

Marian shifted enough to reveal that the ladies had heard of their arrival. He shouldn't have been surprised. Miss Hallowton, who kept the house where they had taken a room, seemed the type to share the news of arrivals.

"We were hoping to run into you," Charles said as the

young man from the auto started down the street towards them. "Would you care for an evening ramble?"

Marian bit at her bottom lip before answering. "Oh, no, we can't. We're going to a writing group."

Charles paused, glancing at Georgette with a frown. "Are you...are you intending to let your neighbors tinker with—"

He cut off his statement when the man from the auto joined them. "Marian, love. Hello again, Miss Marsh! So nice to see you."

"Mr. Parker," Georgette said, her eyes dancing at the sight of the fellow. Charles's own gaze narrowed on the bloke. Just who was this fellow and why was he here?

Marian grinned at the man, resituating herself to put him nearer Georgette as she glanced at Charles and Joseph. "Mr. Aaron, Detective Aaron, allow me to present my cousin, Harrison Parker. He works at my father's company but has the office nearer to us."

Charles noted that he was younger, more in line with Joseph and Georgette than youthful Marian or older Charles. To his irritation, Charles also saw he was one of those sporting types with broad shoulders and rather vivid blue eyes. After a day in the office, the man had a bit of stubble about his jaw. One would think that he'd shave before appearing in public looking quite so ragged.

"Hullo there!" Mr. Parker said, holding out his hand and shaking both of theirs heartily. "Are you going to the writers group as well?"

"Yes," Charles and Joseph said at once, neither needing to look at the other.

"We do need to be going," Georgette said quietly, avoiding Charles's gaze as she glanced towards the library. "I have received strict instructions that I must be early as I volunteered to bring the refreshments."

She gestured with the basket, and that Parker fellow took it from her before Charles could offer. The man offered his arm and Georgette took it, casting a smiling gaze behind her at Charles and Joseph.

Charles followed at Georgette and Parker's heels as she hurried towards the brick building and up the steps. Just before the man could open the door, Charles reached past her to open it himself. Georgette thanked him quietly, and he had to shake himself. The last few times he'd seen her, she'd been in London. He'd forgotten this quieter version of her. She was so firmly entrenched in her Bard's Crook persona, he felt as though he weren't seeing her at all, but a shadow of her instead.

Regardless, however, Parker seemed to be rather intrigued by quiet Georgette.

"Mr. Aaron," Miss Hallowton said as he appeared, frowning past his shoulder as she said again to Joseph, "Mr. Aaron. We were just about to start our writers group. Is there something wrong with your room?"

"We've decided to join the group," Joseph said. "Small town charm, pursuing our passions. Charles works with books, you know."

Charles cleared his throat and lied. "Only peripherally."

"This is a group for serious writers only," Miss Hallowton replied.

"Oh, we're serious," Joseph replied, moving past her before she could stop them. Charles followed quickly, approaching Georgette where she was laying out a basketful of refreshments for the group.

Before he could reach her, Harrison spoke to her. "My cousin tells me you like to dabble with writing as well."

Georgette blushed brilliantly and looked down to the arrangement of her scones and jam.

What a nincompoop, Charles thought. They were attending a writers group. Surely everyone attending was interested in writing.

4

GEORGETTE DOROTHY MARSH

"Why are they here?" Georgette whispered to Marian as she joined her friend at the table. Marian had saved Georgette a seat next to Harrison, but he was trapped at the refreshments table with Virginia Baker.

Miss Hallowton cleared her throat at the head of the table. "I hope you all brought your writing samples. As I have explained to each of you, this is a group for aspiring writers who wish to help each other improve."

Virginia sniffed and pulled a few pages from her handbag. Georgette focused on those sheets of paper. Surely Mrs. Baker did not truly wish to write? Georgette's gaze traveled from Mrs. Baker to Laurieann Schmitz, who had moved to Bard's Crook sometime after the ruckus of Georgette's first book. She had yet to meet the newcomer. Perhaps Georgette should have sought her out when she arrived, but after Charles and Joseph had returned to London, Marian had spent some weeks with her family, and Georgette simply hadn't the will.

Georgette had been left alone in Bard's Crook with a village who still saw her as the same she'd always been, and she'd been relegated to being the mix of the old maid and village idiot. It hadn't fit her as well, and Georgette had found solace in writing The Secrets of Harper's Bend and Josephine Marie.

The fact that Josephine Marie was purely imaginative wasn't quite true. It was far more imaginative than the Harper's Bend stories, but Josephine Marie was also where Georgette had grappled with how she felt about the murder. She was very much afraid that the pieces of herself she'd put in Josephine Marie would reveal her as Joseph Jones. Even the name was something of a clue and that was before the reader discovered the plot of a woman who had innocently caused the death of another. In truth, Josephine Marie was a self-reflective look into Georgette's heart that revealed her for anyone who cared to see.

Georgette's fingers trailed over her own pages, her gaze following her fingers until she glanced up. Charles was directly across from her. She told herself to return to calling him Mr. Aaron. Those early days of their friendship had passed, and despite what Marian and Eunice said, the Misters Aaron were either in Bard's Crook for the reason they'd stated or they were here to get to know Marian better.

Georgette found that Charles's gaze had turned to hers while she'd been lost in her thoughts, entirely missing whatever Miss Hallowton had said. Georgette glanced around the group and saw that people were taking notes. She really must stop getting lost in her thoughts. It had become something of a terrible problem since she had written that first book.

He tilted his head at her and then said to Miss Hallowton, cutting into her lecture on how things would work, "I will provide feedback to Miss Marsh."

Miss Hallowton's mouth dropped. It was evident she was upset that she'd been interrupted but also baffled by Mr. Aaron's claim.

Harrison shifted next to Georgette, and she glanced his way. He looked perturbed, but he might have actually believed Marian's tales that Georgette could somehow help him with his stories.

"Unless," Charles said, "you were intending to already work with someone else this week?"

"No," Georgette said vaguely. "No, of course not."

"Yes, well," Mrs. Baker cut in, "now that we have that worked out, I am counting on you, my dear Harrison, to assist me with my little story." She laughed lightly, echoed by Marian who wasn't even trying to hide her snicker. "Oh, did I say something funny?"

"I'd be happy to work with you," Harrison agreed, though his tone didn't quite convey his statement as truth.

Georgette glanced down at her hands to hide her twitching mouth. Harrison must have realized that Mrs. Baker had turned her acquisitive gaze his way and was unsure he wanted to succumb. She was rather older than him.

"Who will work with me?" Miss Schmitz asked, holding up a pile of papers. "I've decided to take note of this Joseph Jones and write about Bard's Crook."

The room fell to stark silence, dramatized by Marian

31

giggling into her hand. Georgette elbowed her friend when no one was looking their way, but Marian just whispered a tearful, "I'm sorry. It's just...it's just..."

Ridiculous in the extreme, Georgette thought.

"Why would you want to duplicate that fiend?" Miss Hallowton snapped. "Sending good British women off on adventures. I had to assure my superior I had no intentions of packing my bags and heading to...to...Albania."

"I believe he sent you to Cypress," Marian added, pretending to helpfulness as Georgette carefully sipped her tea. The devil was in her gaze when she turned to Miss Schmitz and asked, "Why do you care what Joseph Jones did? You moved here after the books."

"The first book, yes," Miss Schmitz said. "I am clearly Caroline Hardport in the second book."

Georgette sat up straighter at that and wasn't quite able to bite back, "I'm sorry?"

"Surely you see it?" Miss Schmitz asked. "We're both new to the town, independent, observant women." She grinned as she added, "Of course, Mr. Jones took some liberties with my character, but artistic types don't see the way we mere mortals do."

"I'm afraid I don't see it," Marian replied between giggles. "Miss Hardport was the new librarian. You aren't a librarian."

"But I am the only new person in Bard's Crook who isn't one of the boarders."

"Miss Hardport listens at doors and entangles herself in the affairs of the new Alvin family along with several other families. She's something of a bedeviler," Marian said. "Why would you see yourself as the villain in the piece?"

"Clearly Mr. Jones took liberties with more than just

where Miss Hallowton might travel. If you do leave, my dear Miss Hallowton, I would be interested in your position. These are hard times and we do what we must. I'm sure my people never imagined I'd be needing to work someday."

"That was fiction, and I have no intention of leaving Bard's Crook!" Miss Hallowton snapped. "Enough of this nonsense about that...that damned book. Impetus though it might be for this group, we need not linger our thoughts or energies on it."

Georgette nibbled her bottom lip at that statement, staring in surprise at Miss Hallowton and fighting the urge to ask for clarification. Charles saved her the trouble. "What do you mean that the book was an impetus?"

"Whoever this Joseph Jones is," Miss Hallowton said waspishly, "he is one of us. If he can do it then why not us?" Her gaze flicked from Mrs. Baker to Miss Marsh and then she amended, "Well, those of us with the wit and the will."

Georgette smiled vaguely, but inside she was flabbergasted. Was Miss Hallowton daring to pursue a dream because of Georgette's success? Was it possible that she hadn't only caused a murder but given a few rays of hope? There was something about seeing someone else's success at a similar dream and think, If that person can do it, so can I. If Georgette were a little kinder, she might have reached out to Miss Hallowton to provide encouragement, but it seemed Georgette wasn't quite that kind.

"Ah," Charles said, clearing his throat. "Surely we aren't just going to discuss that book and whoever you think you might be in it? I should very much like to continue on. I assume we trade papers and then discuss the piece? Miss Marsh, shall we?" He rose and held out his hand and Georgette followed, taking his arm while he led them to a table in the corner of the library.

A few steps in, and she returned for her teacup and scone with a grin at Charles. He was the only one who could see it, and he'd heard of her tea indulgences since he'd bought her first book. In the meetings since their first, he'd taken to asking her about her latest splurges.

They sat across from each other with her piece in front of him. "Is this the third book?"

"It's something new."

"How is the third book going?"

She pressed her lips together. "I—"

His head cocked. "Have you talked yourself out of the reviews being accurate? You're worried about it? Really, Miss Marsh," he chided, "after two books that the world loves?"

She shrugged. "Each book makes it more and more—" she glanced over her shoulder and then whispered, "fictional. I have little faith in my ability to write without their help and yet...I suppose I must. It is too painful for them when I write about this village. It was never supposed to be like that. I never imagined they'd see what I'd done or recognize themselves in it."

"I think you'll discover that you were always writing without their help, my dear Georgette. Eventually, you'll have faith in what you have done. Surely you trust me to tell you what I think? I promise that my affection for you will not affect the businessman you see before you."

"I—"

He smiled at her, a gentle thing that no one had ever given her. It was as though he saw her and saw she was something that needed to be protected. She wasn't, in fact, all that sure he was accurate there. She had been surviving all this time with only Eunice. It just seemed when it was the two of them, like this, discussing her books, that she brought out that gentleness in him.

She shook off the silly thought and imagined that he was rather kind and cajoling with his newer authors.

"Now what have you been up to?"

She blushed. "I have two books done. A few shorter things while I was trying to find my footing with something that was entirely invention."

"But the books?"

She paused. "The Secrets of Harper's Bend and one I named, Josephine Marie."

"Georgette, have you been keeping secrets from me?" Charles glanced down in utter delight at the manuscript in front of him. "Is this it? Is this Josephine Marie? Oh heavens, woman, I didn't dare to hope even for a full third book by now. And you were going to let them tinker with these? I could wring your neck."

"They're a writers group, Mr. Aaron. I'm hardly a skilled author. I'm an...an...inexplicably successful dilettante, and no, that is one of my short pieces."

"Who said you were a dilettante and why did you believe them?" He shook his head to answer himself and said with surprising earnestness, "Trust me, my dear Georgette, I have read the musings and attempts of thousands of dilettantes. You might not be a very experienced author, but you are a very good one. One of the best it has been my pleasure to come across, and if I have to snatch these books away from you to keep them from this group of dabbling, unaccomplished amateurs, I will do so."

Georgette would have smiled if she were a little more

comfortable. She'd have apologized for the wild gaze in Mr. Aaron's gaze but assumed all that worry was for the book he needed for his business.

Another thought struck her, and she shook it off. She was still hearing the echo of Eunice and Marian swearing that Mr. Aaron had come to Bard's Crook to pursue some sort of relationship with her, and she couldn't believe such nonsense. She wouldn't entertain the folly of such idiocy and allow herself to be distracted by ridiculous fantasies.

Mr. Aaron leaned back, lifting the pages she'd brought, and began reading. Georgette stared at him, then rose. If she watched him, she'd analyze every move, every twitch on his face, every expression. If he laughed, she'd want to desperately wonder what part he was laughing at and if it was the situation she'd created or poor writing.

She left him at the table, and he didn't seem to notice. He was absorbed into what she'd written with a small smile on his face. Georgette nibbled her thumb as she walked away. Nothing about this evening—that she'd been almost terrified to attend—was going as she expected. Could she trust Mr. Aaron to give her feedback on her writing? She needed to...she wasn't sure.

She needed more tea and would have preferred some of the new blend she'd purchased with the coffee beans and cocoa beans. She had been thinking since she'd finished her first cup that she really did need another.

"What are you doing over here?" Marian hissed as Georgette poured herself another cup of the very good Earl Grey tea she'd brought along. She made herself a second scone, putting too much clotted cream on it to go with the too much cream in her teacup.

"You know I don't like to watch people read my stories,"

Georgette whispered back, glancing around the library. Miss Schmitz was working with Miss Hallowton. Mr. Hadley, the herbalist, was the odd man out, looking after Miss Hallowton with a distressed gaze. "That is what true longing looks like."

"You put that in your book," Marian said. "That longing. It made me weep more than once."

"Everyone feels that longing. You weep because you recognize it and feel it yourself," Georgette replied. "As though some piece of yourself is missing. I think it's why people believe in love."

"You don't?" Marian asked, her gaze wide and searching as it darted over Georgette's face.

She squeezed Marian's hand. "Not everyone gets a happily-ever-after, Marian. I'm not holding my breath for some fairytale that will never happen for me." Her gaze was clear and uncompromising as she added, "I know what I am."

"That's"—Marian reached out, taking Georgette's hand—"a sad story, and you know it isn't—" She stopped, studying Georgette. "I'm not really sure you do know."

Georgette laughed as she patted Marian's cheek. "You aren't looking at it right, love. We count the blessings we have, not the ones we don't. You had better get back to your Detective Aaron. He's looking this way."

"He's not the only one," Marian replied, glancing first at her cousin and then at Charles.

"He just finished the story. I'll go get my feedback, shall I?"

5

Once again, the goddess Atë turned her sly gaze on Bard's Crook. She liked the village even more than the fictional version, Harper's Bend. Once again, it seemed that Harriet Lawrence, the widow, was called to the wood. She wandered for long hours, and on her way back, she discovered—not for the first time—Miss Schmitz scribbling into a notebook near the very spot where Harriet's husband had died.

Harriet's brows lifted at the sight, hating the image more than she knew possible. What was the chance that the location was selected innocently? As she stared towards the spot, she remembered the last way she'd seen him. He'd struck her hard, and she'd been holding her cheek, looking back at him from where the force had made her spin. His eyes were alight with fire and fury, and she'd kept her hand to her face and ran. She'd hated him then and death hadn't changed a thing.

Her brows drew low, and she pressed her hand to her cheek once again. She spun, running towards her home, bypassing the herbalist, Mr. Hadley. He had also been watching Miss Schmitz. He'd seen her more than once about the village, and she'd been slowly making him take notice. He'd seen her near the library, and when she'd left, Miss Hallowton had frowned after. He'd seen Miss Schmitz laughing as she spoke with Mrs. Thornton, but Mrs. Thornton had looked concerned. To see Miss Schmitz now, there?

He remembered all too well the sight of Lawrence dead on the ground. The feel of carrying his body to the doctor's auto. The fact that someone was using the location to scribble inane thoughts into a journal was too much for the good Mr. Hadley.

Her location and her manner was helping Miss Schmitz to rise in the wily goddess's affection. Atë's affections could be so easily swayed. In the week since The Further Adventures of Harper's Bend's release, Miss Schmitz had told anyone who would listen that the author had based the shrew, Caroline Hardport, off of herself.

Of course, anyone who knew the details behind the book knew that Georgette had completed it before the woman had even arrived in Bard's Crook. Miss Schmitz hadn't taken into account that as soon as the first book was finished, the author would have turned her attention to the next book. The book had to have been done for months to have been published in the last week.

For someone like Dr. Wilkes, who knew a bit about publishing, he simply laughed and changed the subject to discover the mischief of his boys rather than the mischief of a lonely woman with no family. For someone like Marian Parker, who had read the book once, after much pleading, and before Miss Schmitz had moved to Bard's Crook, the claim was a great joke. For a few, however, they were far less pleased. Just who was this Joseph Jones and how did he prognosticate such things? Perhaps through a woman like Schmitz, using her beady little eyes to ferret out their secrets.

GEORGETTE DOROTHY MARSH

For Georgette Dorothy Marsh, however, the claim was something of a conundrum. Was Miss Hardport not irritating? Did she not cause trouble and pain? Perhaps Georgette had created a heroine when she'd wanted to create a villainess. Perhaps Georgette had failed at her intentions, and she should re-examine what she had done versus what she'd intended and do it better next time.

Georgette spent the morning after her first writers group reading over The Further Adventures of Bard's Crook looking for a reason why Miss Schmitz would see herself in that book. She skimmed the pages, remembering the book she'd half-forgotten while writing the next two books. It didn't seem she'd written the character wrong. Was that because she knew what she'd been trying to convey? If only she could read it as though she hadn't written it and discover what she'd done wrong.

"I don't understand it," Georgette said finally as she closed the volume and placed it on the table next to her.

"You don't understand that Miss Schmitz wants to see

herself in Hardport?" Eunice asked, crossing the kitchen to refill Georgette's teacup. It made Eunice quite happy to see her girl filling out in her face. She pushed the cream towards Georgette, and Miss Georgie topped off her teacup with an excess of cream and sugar, making Eunice smile to herself. Her girl always did have a bit of a sweet tooth. Today was a day, she thought, for making cakes. Especially if those Aaron men were in town. Sooner or later, they'd be appearing at the door with one excuse or another.

Georgette hummed as she nodded and then sipped that odd tea she'd purchased. Who combined cocoa beans, coffee beans, and tea? Odder and odder. It quite made Eunice think of that Wonderland book she'd read Georgette when she was a girl.

"You should go for a walk, Miss Georgie, before you start working. You work too much and walk too little. It's not good for you. Get some air. Stretch your legs. Don't come back until you've winded yourself a bit or your lungs will quit working properly."

Georgette rose and kissed Eunice on the cheek as soon as the tea was finished. "You take such good care of me. You'd think I could do it, seeing as how I'm supposedly a fully grown, modern woman. Yet, it seems without you, my dresses would be dirty, my hair askew, and my hips hurting from working too long."

"If your hips are hurting," Eunice said dryly, "then walk longer, and take those mongrels of yours."

Georgette whistled to her dogs and exited the back of her cottage. There was a trail at the back of her garden that led through a nearby green and onto the lane that led to the wood. Georgette made her way, entirely missing Mr. Aaron approaching her door with his hat in his hand and her manuscripts under his arm.

He'd talked her into handing them over the previous night. He'd known he was being pushy and done it all the same. She had caved, as he'd known she would. He stayed up late reading and making notes. Joseph had been forced to cover his face with his pillow. If only Miss Hallowton had two rooms to spare.

The boy could suffer if Charles could, and if his Georgie wanted true feedback, he'd give it to her. He loved her works as they were. The artlessness and honest way she told her stories was as charming as the stories themselves.

Charles had gone through the manuscripts, making notes for her and praying he wasn't ruining a good thing. He was nervous to hand them over. She was such a quiet thing. He'd had to give himself quite a pep talk about her. She could handle feedback. It wasn't all negative. It wasn't even really negative at all. More coaching. He took care to point out the parts where she was particularly charming, but he didn't want to crush her by noting the weaker points too harshly. She seemed somehow to be both a delicate flower and a stalwart oak.

He took a deep breath and rapped his knuckles against the door. There were no sounds of barking, and he glanced about, looking for those dogs she'd rescued. The only sign was a basket of tennis balls near the door.

After a minute and a second knock, a harried-looking Eunice opened the door. Her gaze narrowed on him and she put her hands on her hips as she huffed out a breath. "You're too late."

"Whatever do you mean?"

"She re-read that book of hers, drank too much tea, and

let me shoo her out the door. If you didn't pass her, you missed her."

"Did she say where she was going?"

"Just to take those dogs of hers for a walk. I scolded her to get herself well and truly winded, so perhaps she went towards the wood. She's got a fair bit on her mind."

"That Parker fellow?"

Eunice just stared and then snorted. "Her books. She doesn't trust herself. Who can blame the girl when everyone treats her like the village idiot? She's worried that because the fool Schmitz sees herself as the villain that somehow my miss made a mistake in her writing and made someone appealing who was supposed to be otherwise."

Charles shook his head, as baffled as Eunice. "Fool woman is right." His thoughts returned immediately to Georgie. He knew she was quiet, and he'd seen her when she'd been at her worst. Bone thin, in too-large, threadbare clothes, but her looks had improved as the worries had faded.

"I feel as though I'm blindfolded here, Eunice. I wonder if you'd let me ask you a few questions."

"No."

Charles stared, stunned at the denial. He'd rather thought Eunice liked him. "I could use some help."

"You could if you're here for what I think you are." Charles was shocked to feel a burning in his cheeks that only intensified as Eunice added, "You think you could have her for the taking. She'll tell you she's Charlotte Lucas"—Eunice made sure he got the reference before she continued—"letting in any man who wants her for the taking, but she's not, you know."

"I know," he said, but he realized he'd treated her just

that way, making sure that there wasn't a better female available, reviewing the field is what he'd told himself. He felt a flash of shame. Georgette Dorothy Marsh was far more to him than something to set aside. He had to admit —he'd panicked a little at the idea of actually getting married.

"She's a good girl. She's smart, clever, and hard-working. Her books are good. She doesn't need anyone to save her. Never did, really. I think you'll discover she's been learning she isn't Charlotte Lucas."

"I am not Mr. Collins," Charles said.

"But," Eunice asked with a waspish tone, "are you Mr. Darcy?" She shut the door.

Charles blinked at the closed door. There was a piece of him that noted it had been painted a cheery mustard yellow. He glanced around, taking in the cut verge, the flowers blooming in pots. The whitewashed fence and the fresh coat of paint on the cottage. He supposed he knew what she'd done with the second cheque he'd written her for the next round of royalties.

He sighed and stepped away from the cottage, exiting the garden as Miss Parker and her cousin appeared, a dog gamboling around them. It seemed that Joseph was having the same luck as Charles. He lifted his hand and forced a grin while he took in the man walking at Miss Parker's side.

"Hello there!" Marian called. "How lovely to see you, Mr. Aaron. Lovely day and all that."

Parker nodded to Charles from behind his cousin, his gaze moving to the cottage and then back to Charles.

"I'm afraid Miss Marsh doesn't seem to be at home," Charles told them.

"She must have taken that back trail to the wood.

Eunice has been pushing her out the door now that the days are sunnier. I suppose she did spend much of the last round of rainy months busy with her tinkering."

So, Parker didn't realize that Georgette was a writer. Not a real writer.

"Tinkering?" Parker asked.

Marian only shrugged and then reached past him to point out a wood warbler. "I do love their pretty yellow feathers. Don't you?"

Parker didn't see his cousin's sidestepping, but Charles recognized it. Of course, he knew much of the facts about Miss Marsh that Parker hadn't been trusted with. It was absurd, Charles thought, how much he liked that.

Humility struck him a moment later when he realized that the only reason Charles knew her secrets was because she'd sent her book to his office. Would she have trusted him if she hadn't chosen his name from the list of publishers?

He had no idea. Charles glanced at Marian, who was watching him far too carefully.

"It's interesting, isn't it?" she said low so that Parker, who had picked up a ball to throw for Marian's dog, didn't hear. "When you realize there are whole worlds behind her eyes that she's not sharing with you."

"Why did she go for a walk?"

"She didn't think you'd come."

"Why?" Charles ran his hand over his hair. "Of course I was coming."

"Why should she?" Marian snapped, not hiding a flash of fury. "You left for London. You made no promises. You carried her off like a knight in shining armor and then you went back to your work. You know what makes me the angriest? That's what she expected. She deserves better."

Marian whistled for her dog and gave him a cheeky wave as though she hadn't just scolded him. She called a cheery goodbye that was all lies and turned her back on him.

6

GEORGETTE DOROTHY MARSH

The walk to the wood was just what Georgette needed to clear her head. She was almost positive that she'd written Miss Hardport as an interfering gossip who attempted to destroy people's lives with her machinations. Therefore, it must be for another reason that Miss Schmitz identified herself in the book. Was it possible that Miss Schmitz was that type of interfering busybody, and the similarities were just a very odd coincidence?

Georgette's mind moved from Miss Schmitz to her current books. She had finished her Secrets and her Josephine Marie, at least as much as she could before she got feedback. She hadn't had to make major changes to the last two books. Charles might not suggest many changes to these two either. That wasn't what she wanted. She wanted to get better as a writer.

She sighed and pulled out the list she'd tucked into her pocket to look at it. It was a simple enough list. She'd been able to afford much of what had been on it. She'd replaced much of her wardrobe, she'd replaced her furniture, indulged in teas, painted the outside of her cottage. In a time when many were saving the scraps of vegetables and making bone soup, Georgette had been blessed enough to escape financial doom.

Her list was dwindling. She needed to replace some things in her bedroom and freshen the paint inside of her cottage, but she'd wait until late summer to do those things. She had determined to save every last half-penny of her next book sales, barring tea indulgences, in order to feel as though she didn't have to write. It wasn't that she intended to stop, she simply wanted to know that if Mr. Aaron stopped buying her books, she and Eunice would still survive.

The walk took her past Mr. Hadley, who stopped her. "I wonder, Miss Marsh, if I might have a word."

Georgette hid her shock as she nodded, giving him a vague smile.

"I find that I am concerned," he said. "I—I—know that you're good friends with Miss Parker."

"Yes," Georgette said quietly.

"Do you know...ah—do you think... Oh, I find...perhaps I better just..." Mr. Hadley's face had flushed and then he said all at once, "Do you believe that Mr. Harrison Parker is attending the writers group to gather Miss Hallowton's personal attention?"

Georgette stared blankly at Mr. Hadley for a moment. Miss Hallowton was all edges and elbows and she was forty if she was a day. Harrison Parker, on the other hand, was a vital man somewhere in his late twenties. Mr. Parker might have some purpose to his attendance at that writers group, but Georgette was certain it wasn't a relationship with Miss Hallowton.

"Ah," she said carefully, "no."

"She's very lovely," Mr. Hadley told Georgette as though persuading her to see Miss Hallowton as a love interest for a much younger man.

"She's quite clever too," Georgette added kindly, "to think up and arrange that group, and when she works so hard."

Mr. Hadley nodded and then pushed his spectacles up on his nose. "I fear that I am a bit protective of her. You understand. She's a woman alone."

Georgette stared at him for a moment, wondering if he realized he was talking to her—a woman alone—younger and arguably in more need of protection, and yet he seemed blind to the very idea that Georgette might have longed for, even prayed for, that very thing. It seemed that she was, in fact, chopped liver. She wanted to scold herself, but there was very little time for that with his anxious gaze fixated on her. She was, she realized, a cipher to him and nothing more.

"I believe, from his cousin, that Mr. Parker is a very serious amateur writer."

"Is he?" Mr. Hadley's gaze widened with something akin to sheer joy blended with relief. "How lovely."

"Miss Parker tells me that Mr. Parker has written more than one book and is attending the writers group to improve his writing and for no other reason."

"Is he really?" Mr. Hadley huffed out a breath. "Oh, thank you, Miss Marsh. Thank you ever so much."

Georgette stared after him as he hurried back into the wood. No doubt he was going to check on a patch of this plant or another. Susan rubbed against Georgette's leg and whined low in her throat. Leaning down to give the dog a good love pat, Georgette said, "It's not like I wanted him for myself."

Susan licked Georgette's hand and then pushed up on her back legs to lick Georgette's face.

"It's just sometimes even I want someone to long for me."

The dog panted happily in Georgette's face, and she laughed. "Maybe," Georgette told the dog, "even love me as you do, my darling."

With a near frantic combination of kisses and tail-waggling, Susan, Bea, and Dorcas didn't so much make Georgette feel better as help her slide back into the same resigned position she'd achieved almost before she was old enough to be wed and dream of love.

She made her way out of the wood and down one of the less busy lanes towards her cottage. She would, she thought, take a journal and a pen to the teashop, enjoy a good cuppa, and keep out of Eunice's hair.

It would be rather luxurious to spend an afternoon having Mrs. Yancey wait on Georgette and serve her up liver pâte and cucumber sandwiches with petit fours and shortbread biscuits, perhaps even some of the early strawberries. Luxurious or not, Georgette was going to do it regardless. She had heard from Marian that they were serving a new blend of tea that Georgette wanted to try.

Georgette hurried into the cottage, calling to Eunice that she'd decided to try the tea at Yancey's.

"Good idea, love," Eunice said. "Mrs. Wilkes told me that they have delightful little cakes there too. Make sure you order some after that walk. You need to keep your strength."

Georgette stuck her head out of her bedroom door. "You told me to walk until I got winded. I obeyed, I promise, and now I need to remedy that? Perhaps I should have lolled about in my bed and saved myself the effort of the walk and the cakes."

Eunice put her hands on her hips and lifted a brow. "After all that working you've been doing, Miss Georgie, I might've cheered if you did. What I wanted was something other than you banging away at that typewriter of yours. "

"Liar," Georgie gasped with a wink. She returned to her room, filled a pitcher with water and then ran a cloth over her lips and face. She dabbed lavender perfume by her ears and put on one of her nicer day dresses. It was so very rare for her to indulge like this that Georgette was determined to enjoy it to the fullest. She even dabbed some soft pink lipstick on her lips and pulled her hair back with a rather pretty barrette.

Georgette hurried down the stairs in her dress. It was nice enough to only need her cream cardigan to keep her warm.

"You look nice, love," Eunice said. "How pretty you are is more and more apparent as you age."

Georgette rolled her eyes at the compliment, laughing it off. "Darling, you see through loving eyes. Trust me, I'm as plain as I've always been. As for dressing up, other than when I'm making my little trips into London or going to church, I don't get a chance to dress up for anything. A tea out seems like just the thing. I think I'll go get Marian and see if she'd like to come."

Georgette walked to Marian's home but found her friend hadn't returned yet. She paused to ask Mrs. Parker about her health and listened to stories of her children and grandchildren. When the long-winded answer to how she was came to an end, Mrs. Parker glanced Georgette over and lifted her brows. "You look rather nice for a ramble."

"I'm going to try the new teashop," Georgette admitted, "on something of a whim."

"Marian will be sad she missed it." Mrs. Parker's gaze narrowed and she added, "You don't look like yourself."

"Blame your Marian," Georgette replied quietly. "She's been influencing the things I've purchased."

"That's not it," Mrs. Parker said, and she leaned back and clucked to herself. "I'm not sure what it is. You look nice, Georgette." It wasn't a compliment. It was more baffled confusion. "It's makeup, isn't it? In my day, women took the looks God gave them and didn't try to pull one over on the world."

Georgette smiled and hurried away. She didn't need anyone thinking too much about her, even if they were jumping to the wrong conclusions. Their analysis and attention made her feel uncomfortable. It seemed that after years of being overlooked, having someone focus on you was even more distressing than being ignored.

<hr />

"MISS MARSH!" SOMEONE CALLED AS GEORGETTE

rounded the corner of the building housing the teashop. If it wasn't Miss Schmitz, who'd occupied much of Georgette's thoughts that morning. The woman caught up. "Hello, dear."

"Miss Schmitz," Georgette said, surprised as she reached for the teashop door. Dear was rather familiar, wasn't it, after having just met in a group setting. "Good afternoon."

"Oh!" Miss Schmitz's blue eyes narrowed on Georgette and then they widened with delight. "We can have tea together!"

Georgette winced, glancing about as though Marian or even Charles would appear. No one rescued her, so she followed the woman to the table, seeing with surprise that Mrs. Hanover avoided Miss Schmitz's gaze and didn't greet Georgette at all. Had she done something? Georgette stared at Mrs. Hanover as she rose, leaving the establishment with money on the table, and her tea half-finished.

What in the world? Georgette would have worried that her status as Joseph Jones had gotten out, but she hadn't put Mrs. Hanover in her story. To be perfectly honest, the woman was so very normal that there had been nothing to put in the story. She'd have been nothing more than a shadow in the background of more interesting 'characters.'

"Don't worry about Martha," Miss Schmitz said cheerily, "she's a tad upset with me, I think. It'll smooth over."

Georgette blinked in shock. There was certainly no possible way that Martha Hanover had given this woman permission to use her first name as though they were lifelong friends.

Moments later, Georgette watched the teashop proprietress, who crossed to the table and took their order without her customary kindness. Before Georgette could order the blend she'd heard of, Miss Schmitz said, "We'll share a pot of your English breakfast tea. I can't stand those odd blends, don't you agree, dear? A good English breakfast tea or an Earl Grey if I must try something different."

Georgette nibbled her bottom lip as Miss Schmitz continued. "Some of your brown bread and butter. That will be all."

It was just so...so...rudely said. This was Mrs. Yancey. Georgette liked the woman. Unlike so many, she'd never made Georgette feel like a simpleton. She tried to convey her apology to Mrs. Yancey by look alone, and the proprietress nodded slightly and then turned silently and returned to her kitchens.

"I—" Georgette was at an utter loss for words. "I—"

"I know your secret," Miss Schmitz said exultantly. Her blue eyes trapped Georgette with a brilliant shining light that made Mrs. Baker's avarice seem like a candle about to sputter out.

"I—" Georgette forced herself to clear her mind. If her secret was known, all was not lost. She would be okay. Somehow, all would be fine. But then reason struck her and instead of begging for silence, she said, "I can't imagine that you do."

Miss Schmitz grinned with rather sharp teeth. Odd that Georgette hadn't noticed those before. "Yet, now I know you have one. It won't take long for me to figure it out. I'm clever like that."

A rush of fury loosened Georgette's tongue in a way that she rarely allowed herself. Pushing to her feet, Georgette looked down at the woman. "I'm not sure why you are intent on trying to cause me pain, but I won't help you. You aren't Caroline Hardport. The author did not base that character on you, and your attempt to act as the woman in that book shows you to be of even lesser moral fortitude. To look at a...at a...villainess and want to be like her? Of all the ridiculous things! You should be ashamed of yourself, madam!"

Georgette crossed to Mrs. Yancey. "I apologize that I was in any way involved with that treatment of you."

"Dressing down that foolish, evil woman made my day, Miss Marsh. Seeing that has brightened this infernal day."

Georgette smiled, squeezing her hand as she heard the whispers behind her with Miss Schmitz saying loudly, "She doesn't know one thing about publishing or that book. I'd be shocked if she'd even read it. What utter cheek to declare something like fact that she can't possibly know. I'd heard she was simple, but my goodness—"

Georgette took a deep breath in and refused to react to that...that...shrew. "I should very much like to order some of your lavender earl grey tea blend," she said to Mrs. Yancey, "and your new specialty blend for my home, and if you would be so good to wrap up some of your petit fours and cakes for Eunice and myself, I'd be ever so grateful." When Miss Schmitz's complaining only got louder, Georgette said evenly, "I'll be waiting outside."

Georgette stormed from the teashop and stopped on the pathway just outside the doors. She took in another deep breath and then slowly let it out. She very rarely allowed herself to get well and truly angry, and her fingers were shaking. She needed...she needed...she needed to walk this off.

The girl who worked at the shop carried out the package and Georgette blinked. "I'll send Eunice over in the morning to pay. I'm sorry, I can't go back in there."

The girl nodded and muttered something that Georgette didn't try to catch. She had little doubt it reflected her own feelings given the sour look on the girl's face. It certainly had to match the one on Georgette's. She nodded and hurried away, cakes and teas in hand.

7

CHARLES AARON

She was storming down the street. If this had been one of her books, she might have described the way her skirt snapped at her rather lovely calves. Or perhaps she'd have focused on the flush on her cheeks and the way her freckles stood out as if they'd darkened with her anger. He thought, however, she'd have focused on the way her delicate hands curled into fists and then splayed over and over again as though she wanted to hit something but wasn't quite sure how to go about it.

If she was lovely when she dropped her guard and let her thoughts flood the gates of her mouth and her expression enliven, she was a smack on the back of the head when angry. He'd been thinking for a while now that she was lovelier than anyone first thought. As if her beauty snuck up on you and once you saw it, you couldn't unsee it. With cheeks flushed, flashing eyes, and heaving bosom, she made you realize what an idiot you were. Quietly lovely? Hardly anything so simple as that. Her looks were quiet. Her features were delicate rather than dramatic. Her coloring was soft and almost muted, but when you paid attention you noticed the lovely, early rose color of her cheeks offset by the peach undertone of her skin and the slightly honey color to her lips. Her eyes weren't dramatic or large or flashing—usually—but all the same, they were varied in color. Not just medium brown but as though they'd been shot through with gold and bronze.

Charles snorted at himself. Look at him waxing poetic over her admittedly lovely eyes. He needed to do more, he thought, than think on her looks and her talents. He needed to consider whether—together—they wouldn't be ideal.

Before he could step into the street to speak to her, that fiend, Parker, beat Charles to it. "Miss Marsh," Parker said.

Georgette paused, staring at him with those flashing eyes and Charles noted the poleaxed look on Parker's face. Before now, the man hadn't truly seen her. It wasn't much of a comfort given that Georgette had no idea how either of them felt about her. She stared at Parker, and Charles was glad to see that she wasn't glad to see the lad. If anything, drawing her attention in the midst of her fury irritated her.

That didn't mean, however, that he'd stay in her poorer graces. He was a handsome enough fellow, and Georgette wasn't used to attention. Would she succumb because of her naiveté? If Parker was serious about Georgette, however, Charles had to decide—right then—if he was.

The field had been surveyed, he'd tried on the usual fare for size and found them wanting. Wanting—that was the word, he thought. That was the word for Georgette. And not in that she was found wanting, but she had somehow taught him to want just by being herself without expectations.

Charles took a deep breath and stepped into the road with one thought in his mind: All was fair in love and war.

"My dear Georgie," he said with a grin, holding out his arm, "there you are."

She blinked stupidly at him, but it didn't matter that she was flummoxed. The key was that Parker's gaze was fixated on Charles and not her. Slowly, she placed her hand on his elbow and acquiesced to his insinuation that they had made plans.

"Are you ready for our walk?"

She stared at him and then nodded a little helplessly, but she turned to Parker, giving him one of those sweet smiles of her that wasn't the vague imitation she normally used with the people from this village. "Did you need something, Mr. Parker? Is Marian looking for me? I did come by your great-aunt's house earlier today to see her."

"It seems you were like ships passing in the night today, Miss Marsh." Parker smiled at her with those white, even teeth, drawing attention to his square jaw, the flashy fellow. "I'll have her find you later. Will you be going home soon?"

"Yes," Georgette said hesitantly, glancing at Charles for confirmation. Parker's gaze followed and narrowed on Charles. It was possible that the look he gave Parker was smug. Charles had no objections to walking her home as long as it was he who was walking her home.

"I'm sure I'll be seeing you soon, Miss Marsh," Parker said, nodding at Charles with a challenge in his eyes before he stepped away.

Georgette looked up at Charles with lifted brows and he

grinned before he admitted, "I suppose I should apologize for manhandling your afternoon, Georgette."

"It's quite all right. I do need to talk to you about something."

"However can I help?"

"Do you recall Laurieann Schmitz from the writers group?"

He frowned for a moment. "The one who thinks she's Miss Hardport in your book?"

Georgette nodded and then told him of her interaction with the woman, finishing with her threat to find out Georgette's secrets.

"Living in Bard's Crook and having to hide who I am is already so difficult, Mr. Aaron. I'm not sure I could stand living here knowing how they hate 'Joseph Jones' and having them realize it was me."

Charles placed his hand over hers on his elbow. It was intoxicating, he thought, for a man to have a pretty woman share her troubles with him. "Am I safe to conclude that only you, I, Eunice, and Marian know of your status?"

"Yes," Georgette said, staring at his hand on hers. She glanced up at him with those honey-brown eyes, shot through with gold. "Mr. Thornton has met you, Mr. Aaron," she reminded him.

"The righteous one?"

Georgette nodded. "Fortunately, he's off right now, visiting his nephew. If anyone realizes who you are, then they'll know who I am."

"They might not," Charles said. "They're not the most insightful of neighbors, my dear. There's no reason, however, to believe that this Miss Schmitz can simply will your secret into the open. Stop speaking of it outside of your house, if you do at all."

Georgette nodded, glancing past him to the green. It was a lovely day. One of those perfect spring days that had blue skies, large puffy white clouds dotting the sky, with just enough chill in the air to keep one from being uncomfortably hot.

"We seem to be quite alone here," Charles said, glancing down at her. Her gaze was so innocent and unprepossessing that he was shocked to realize she had no more idea of him as a lover than she did of Parker. Had he done so little to convey that he liked her more than other women or was she simply so used to being overlooked that she couldn't imagine him thinking of her that way?

"Did you want to talk about books?" She pointed towards the edge of the green where there was a ready bench, and he led her towards it. "I suppose it is safe enough here. She can't come creeping up behind us on the bench there."

"Do you think she would?" Charles asked with a laugh.

"Miss Hardport would," Georgette told him, twisting her mouth. "I know she's a fictional character, and we're discussing a real woman, but somehow she had Mrs. Yancey and Mrs. Hanover unable to hide their dislike. Those women would smile at the devil if he were behaving properly given they've been trained to be polite above all else."

Charles laughed at Georgette's dark aside. He doubted anyone outside of Eunice and Marian saw this side of her, and he was enchanted at the privilege.

"So my books," Georgette said. She glanced at her feet and then admitted, "I'm just not sure of my ability to write purely fiction, but I feel I must all the same. I don't want to keep hurting people with my books."

"It's not you doing those things, Georgette," Charles replied. "You didn't make Evans pick up that cricket bat, and you certainly haven't had anything to do with the Hardport-Schmitz confusion."

She blushed. "I did reread The Further Adventures of Harper's Bend to try to discover why she would see herself in that character. I wasn't very clever, you know, with my descriptions of the first characters. I described them as they looked and behaved, but with Miss Hardport, she was from my head. A mix of half a dozen people and adding up to none of them."

"She reminded me rather strongly of my aunt when I was growing up," Charles admitted. "She too was a single woman. Unlike you, she didn't live her own life but was constantly prying into the lives of others and giving unsolicited and often unkind advice. When Joseph read about Miss Hardport, I spent an entire evening re-telling stories of Aunt Eloise."

Georgette was blushing even deeper, and Charles's head cocked as he looked at her.

"I didn't live my own life, you know. If I had, my book wouldn't have needed to steal so much from others' lives."

Charles wanted to lift her hand and twine their fingers together, but she carried on with her confession before he could.

"After things were going well for me, I realized I had considered myself the protagonist in a novel, like Lizzie Bennet. But I was forced to accept that I was no such thing. I'm only another Charlotte Lucas." Her laugh wasn't even bitter. "Just like her, I was scared and didn't know what to do. Just like her, I'd have accepted the first Mr. Collins who came along."

Charles wasn't able to stop himself from reaching out and taking her hand. "My dear Georgie, you are not Charlotte Lucas. You are so much more than she. She was a foil to make Elizabeth Bennet seem all the more intriguing. You didn't throw yourself at the first Mr. Collins to come along —you picked up your pen and went to work."

"I was lucky," she told him.

"Perhaps," he admitted, "but only to an extent. I'm sure that many novelists have their excellent books overlooked, and you came across Robert's desk when he was desperate to keep searching for something, anything, to prove himself capable of working on his own."

Georgette opened her mouth to object, but Charles stopped her. "Believe me, Georgette," he leaned in and spoke low, "your book sold itself."

"And when it is finally revealed that Joseph Jones is the town's cipher and old-maid Georgette Marsh?" Her eyes were wide with concern and just enough of a sheen to show that she was well and truly worried.

"You aren't trapped here, you know. You could sell your cottage, move to London, to some quaint sea town, to another little village and present yourself from the beginning as who you are rather than allowing the people of this town to continue to confine you within their expectations."

Georgette considered before responding. "I have never, not once, considered living elsewhere. This was always my fate."

"You've changed that once before."

Her eyes brightened as they fixated on him. "I have, haven't I?"

He nodded, still holding her hand and marveling at the softness of her skin. "In a time when so many are suffering, you changed your fate. You are to be commended. What you have done is nearly beyond belief."

She was blushing again, and she twisted the fingers of her free hand in her lap as she considered what he'd said. A moment later, she shook her head, but he wasn't confident that it meant anything other than she was setting the thought aside for the moment.

8

GEORGETTE DOROTHY MARSH

There was too much happening at that moment for her to even process it all. She was worried about Miss Schmitz trying to discover the things Georgette didn't want anyone to know. The idea that she could somehow leave Bard's Crook was rocketing around her mind, and Mr. Aaron was holding her hand. Was he trying to comfort her from her fears? He couldn't possibly mean anything else, could he? Marian would hold Georgette's hand if she were upset.

She looked down at his hand as she played with her fingers in her lap and wondered just what she was supposed to do. Was she supposed to turn her hand over and hold his back? The truth was she wanted to do that more than she could say. She was so often without anyone touching her at all. She wasn't sure how to even interpret what was happening, but one thing she could be sure of, she was an old-maid and he was protective of her as one of his authors. There was nothing else happening here.

She glanced up at him, smiling. "I suppose you should share with me your feedback on the books. Was Josephine Marie very bad?"

She glanced down at their hands again, noting the way his skin was darker than hers. They were rougher as well, and she marveled at the differences between them while trying to hide her fears about her books. He laughed, startling her again with the differences between them. She supposed it was because most people in her life were female, but it was a shockingly deep laugh.

"It was delightful."

She bit down on her bottom lip and then glanced at him once again, trying for a stern tone. "I need to improve as a writer. I have no intentions of being an untutored natural writer. I need feedback to grow."

"Improving sometimes requires feedback. The most important thing is to keep reading and keep writing. Practice and implementing what you see others do—that's the key. Miss Hallowton and that odd Miss Schmitz aren't going to be able to tell you what you might be doing wrong. What you're doing right is natural to you."

"But you could," Georgette told him fiercely, "if you weren't worrying about my feelings and simply helped me without regard to crushing my feelings. I am tougher than I look."

He smiled at her again, and she gaped at him. How could he be a successful businessman and also be so gentle and kind? This was why he was such a good publisher, she thought. He made his writers feel as though each of them were his highest priority. She'd love to meet whichever writer actually fit that bill. What a brilliant fellow he must be.

"I will give you my feedback. I have marked on your books, both of them, the places that I think you were particularly able." She frowned at him, and he held up his hands in surrender. "I find that authors are as blind to when they are doing something well as to when they could improve. Sometimes they need to know when we found parts particularly witty or funny as often as they need to know when we aren't quite sure what they're saying."

Georgette wasn't quite sure she believed him, but she'd take his comments regardless. If nothing else, they'd be a place to start on her improvement.

"You are much surer now." He crossed his legs, letting go of her hand to cross his hands behind his neck and stretch back. "Your Josephine Marie shows that you've grown as a writer. Did you write it before or after The Secrets of Harper's Bend?"

"At the same time."

He cocked his head to glance at her and then turned to face the green again. It was spring and the birds were showing up with greater and greater frequency. There were several pairs flittering around the green, and as he watched them, Georgette thought a sense of peace fell over him.

"I suppose," she mused, "you don't get to enjoy birds quite as often in London."

"Not like this. Plenty of pigeons," he agreed. "There is much to recommend these villages that are close to London. I could see living in one quite happily."

She tried to hide her surprise. She had, of course, put Mr. Aaron into Harper's Bend in her novel, but she never imagined that he'd truly wish to live in such a place. There was something about him, with his nice suit and perfect tie, that proclaimed him as a man about to go to the club for his dinner.

"You convinced me, you know. When you made it work for Mr. Alvin in your book, it made me consider."

She paused as she looked up to reply, but she was distracted by the couple on the edge of the green. If it wasn't the Thornton son and Miss Schmitz! Given the way he was looming over her, Georgette suspected Miss Schmitz just might be trying her same machinations with the man. Georgette couldn't imagine that someone like Jasper Thornton would take the snooping claims of some spinster seriously but that didn't mean the man would take her prying well either.

Charles saw Miss Schmitz with the young man. "What an odd little woman she is. Have I read about this fellow over there?"

"That's one of Thornton's sons," Georgette told him. "They're as aggressive as he can be without being as good."

"What an interesting conundrum to see the titans meet. I can see why you put them in your books. You really do live in the most ridiculous village. What is this?" Charles asked in surprise as Georgette rose.

She looked at him over her shoulder while she stepped away. "I don't want her to see you with me." Georgette tucked her hair behind her ear as he rose to stand near her.

"I think she's distracted."

Georgette glanced at the woman and saw that Jasper Thornton was yelling into Miss Schmitz's face. The wind was blowing the other way, so Georgette couldn't make out what he was saying, but she didn't need to gather the attention of a nefarious woman.

"She might be," Georgette said, stepping from the edge of the green into the wood that ringed it. "I can't risk it. Leaving Bard's Crook?" The very idea gave her a stomach ache. She'd been nowhere. Nowhere at all. To London, to just outside of Lyme for school, to the sea twice with her parents. "I'm not ready. You're the Aaron of Aaron & Luther. It's not an especially hard equation if anyone discovers that and realizes who published Joseph Jones."

There was something in his gaze as she stepped farther into the shadows. "All right. Let's avoid the woman, then. May I walk you home?"

Georgette saw Miss Schmitz had been left staring after Jasper Thornton. Georgette nodded hurriedly and rushed deeper into the wood. They could use the little trail to make their way back to her cottage without being on a busier thoroughfare.

They didn't speak for a few minutes and Georgette finally looked up and admitted, "I suppose I am very cowardly."

"I hardly think so," Charles replied.

"I somehow feel that you are too kind to me, Mr. Aaron."

He reached out and took her hand, placing it on his arm. "I thought we had already agreed on first names, my dear Georgette. I believe I shall cling to yours whether you wish me to or not."

She felt her cheeks blush a brilliant red and she cleared her throat. "Well, yes of course. I suppose we did."

He laughed again. "How about if I invite myself to your house for dinner?"

She nodded rather helplessly, thinking that she had no idea what was happening. He was acting very different this visit, and she wasn't sure what to think of him. Perhaps he was having something of a personal crisis that brought him to Bard's Crook, and she was experiencing him while he was...stumbling?

Why would anyone want to come to Bard's Crook, after all?

"Why don't you bring Detective Aaron, and I will see if I can get Marian to attend. Perhaps the events of the—" Georgette stopped, her head tilting as she witnessed Harriet Lawrence sitting on a stump near one of the wild mushroom patches, weeping into her handkerchief. Georgette paused, worry for the woman striking her. Was this only grief or something else?

She glanced at Charles. "Seven o'clock. Bring your nephew. I must see if she's all right."

Charles might have responded, but Georgette didn't wait long enough to hear it. Instead, she crossed to the crying woman, wondering just what she thought she was doing. There was quite a difference between Harriet having been kind to Georgette to actually being friends. How many times had Georgette looked upon Harriet and Theodora, the doctor's wife, and wished to have been their friend in the place of Virginia Baker, who was neither kind, nor good, nor even a friend.

"Mrs. Lawrence?" Georgette called quietly, dropping to her knees in front of the woman. "Mrs. Lawrence, are you all right?"

"Oh," Mrs. Lawrence said, sniffling. "I'm sorry to bother you, Miss Marsh."

"You aren't bothering me." Georgette took the woman's hands, squeezing them. "Sometimes we need a good cry, but sometimes I think we need to know that people care."

Harriet nodded, her bottom lip trembling. She had plumped up in the months since her husband died. Her face had taken on a pretty glow that you hadn't realized had once been absent. "Thank you, Georgette. I—" She looked down, shaking her head and dabbing away another tear.

Georgette saw that there was a sheet of paper and an envelope at her feet. She carefully picked up the letter, folding it so she didn't see the contents, and then slid it into the envelope. "Did you receive bad news?" Georgette reached back out to take Harriet's hand, squeezing her fingers.

Harriet's watery laugh was bitter. "I suppose I got a rather disturbing missive. Now to decide what to do." She seemed defenseless, which must have been why she looked at Georgette and actually saw her, spoke to her as though she weren't just the old maid that no one liked. "Do you ever feel like if people knew the real you, they'd stop being your friend?"

Georgette must have also been defenseless because for once in her life she answered straightforwardly. "I suppose if I thought that I had true friends, I might worry about losing them should my secrets be revealed. I don't think you have that same worry though, Mrs. Lawrence. You are well-loved, and you have true friends."

Harriet stared at Georgette and then grasped her hand back. "Perhaps you have more friends than you realize."

Georgette pushed to her feet, wrapping her arm through Harriet's as she said, "Let's get you home, shall we? I find a good cup of tea doesn't solve everything, but it does make me feel better."

They walked for some time in silence before Harriet

asked, "Do you truly feel as if you don't have a friend in the world? Surely you don't."

Georgette supposed that having bared her thoughts once, she might do so again. "I know how people see me, Harriet." She didn't know what possessed her to use Harriet's first name, but she didn't regret it. "They see the sad, poor, little old maid that no one loves. Perhaps if someone gets to know me a bit better, they might think 'Oh, that Miss Marsh is so sweet. She's a good girl.' I'm not really, you know. I can be quite unkind."

"I don't believe it," Harriet said. "You are sweet and kind."

Georgette laughed earnestly. "Oh Harriet. Sweet is the word you use for someone that you don't know well enough to know their failings or their thoughts. It's the mask you put over the person who doesn't interest you enough to know better."

"I—"

"Don't let it bother you." Georgette smiled and patted Harriet's hand when they reached the gate to her garden. "I have gotten quite used to being alone. It is, I suppose, a good thing that I've learned to like myself well enough."

"Oh Georgette," Harriet murmured.

"Did you need me to see you inside?"

Harriet shook her head, her eyes wide and fixed on Georgette's face. There was a wrinkle between Harriet's eyes, but Georgette told her, "All will be well, Harriet. Trust in those who love you."

9

GEORGETTE DOROTHY MARSH

"She said you were sweet?" Marian asked as she peeled the potatoes that Eunice had placed in front of her. Georgette was snapping the ends of early green beans as she nodded a reply. "She doesn't know your secret then. I doubt you'd get called sweet after The Chronicles of Harper's Bend and The Further Adventures of Harper's Bend."

"Georgette is sweet," Eunice said from where she was basting a chicken.

"Sometimes," Georgette replied.

"Sometimes," Marian agreed.

Georgette pressed her lips together to hide a smile. "I did sketch out a rather awful scene for Harriet in my next book after talking to her."

"In revenge?" Marian asked, eyes wide. "I thought you liked her."

"No." Georgette finished the last green bean and picked up a knife to help with the potatoes. "More because of the scene where I found her—crying over a letter and asking about losing friends. It made me think of a blackmail plot. The result, I suppose, from watching Miss Schmitz trying to ferret out everyone's secrets. The Secrets of Harper's Bend could follow through with a blackmail plot. Don't you think? Perhaps Miss Hardport will push things to the next level with her secret-gathering. What do you know of Miss Schmitz? She's the oddest little woman."

Marian scraped her potato peel off. "She moved here while I was back at home with my parents. When I came back that introduction party Mrs. Thornton threw for her had already happened. Did you go?"

Georgette shook her head. "I got a rather terrible cold and fever and was sitting with my feet in a bucket of hot water, dirtying handkerchiefs."

Marian leaned back. "Confession time?"

Georgette nodded eagerly.

"I have been avoiding Joseph, using my cousin Harrison, hoping that it would make Joseph jealous."

Georgette gasped and Eunice snorted. "Interesting choice." Eunice's voice was dry.

"I just thought—well," Marian shrugged. "I feel like I'm the jacket Joseph left behind and is coming back for. I'm not even convinced he's come back for me, but to try me on for size. It wasn't like he asked to write to me after he left. Or that he found me in London when I returned. I made sure he knew when I'd be back to London."

"Is that why you came back to Bard's Crook? Because he never came knocking?" Georgette reached out her hand. She could see that Marian had fallen for the handsome detective, and while he hadn't exactly crushed her feelings, he'd bruised them.

"I was tired of looking for him around every corner. He's a detective. Even though he hadn't met my father, it would have been easy for him to meet me again. If he'd wanted to."

"Girls," Eunice told them both as she rubbed the chicken down with herbs and butter. "You can hold a grudge that those men set you aside and then be unhappy. You can spend the rest of your lives wondering what would have happened if you'd been forgiving. Or you can give them a chance to show you matter to them. They did come back, after all."

Georgette didn't believe for a moment that Charles was interested in her in any way but as one of his authors. She was, however, grateful for his feedback. She was only hoping that he'd bring her books when he came.

She dressed for dinner with the same care she'd have dressed for any and then when she met him and his nephew in her parlor, she tried her very best to be her normal self.

Charles and Joseph stayed long enough to try her unique tea mixture with cocoa beans and coffee beans, and her black tea blend. They stayed long enough for Joseph to smoke a cigarette and Charles to smoke his pipe. Georgette took his feedback on her book with the copious notes he'd made for her with glee, and when they left to walk Marian home, Georgette immediately opened the pages.

She skimmed through the notes as she hurried up the stairs. She could do those things he suggested. She could fix the things he'd pointed out. She could sharpen her book. For the first time, she felt as though she knew where to begin. He'd included a list of books for her to consider reading. Eunice called something after Georgette, but she didn't even recognize that the woman had spoken until the office door had already closed.

Georgette put a sheet of paper in the typewriter and glanced down at the pile of pages next to her. A careful restructuring, a focused mind, and she could get the book to Mr. Aaron far sooner than she'd expected.

Georgette wrote through the night and into the next morning until Eunice came into the office and pulled Georgette's chair away from the table.

"You must sleep," Eunice told her.

"I'm too energized to sleep."

"Then you must walk until your mind settles down and then sleep. This isn't good for you, Miss Georgie, and I won't watch you write your health away."

Georgette stared for a moment and then nodded, giving the woman a tight hug. "I can always count on you, Eunice. I don't..." Georgette teared up at the woman, who scowled in return.

"Enough of that."

"But..."

"This is the lack of sleep, Miss Georgie."

"My love for you is not from the lack of sleep," Georgette said with a smirk, "but the tears might be."

"Walk," Eunice ordered.

Georgette started to and then turned back at the doorway. "What if we left Bard's Crook?"

"Left?" Eunice frowned. "Why?"

"Something Harriet Lawrence and Mr. Aaron said." Georgette placed her hand on the doorway and sighed deeply. "If it becomes well known that I am Joseph Jones, living here might be untenable. Harriet's friends would stick with her, I think. But me? I don't have the same loyalty, and I caused so much more mischief than she could possibly have done."

Eunice frowned at the idea. Slowly, she answered, "We might not be giving them enough credit. However, could we do it? Financially?"

Georgette paused, twisting her mouth. The sheer idea made her stomach and her head hurt. It was why she hadn't gone to bed. She'd known she'd only toss and turn. At least by working through the night, she'd been productive.

"Mr. Aaron wants to buy the two books I finished. I think if we saved it all and if we were able to sell the cottage, we'd be well enough off anywhere else. I was thinking of writing a sequel to Josephine Marie. I could write a final Harper's Bend and then maybe, we'd have enough."

Eunice considered. "Might not be a bad idea. I will start going through things and making sure we've fixed everything that might need it. Even if we don't go, it wouldn't be a bad idea to clear out the old things and ensure we do the work over a longer amount of time."

Georgette reached back to squeeze Eunice's hand and then hurried to her bedroom. She'd walk over to the teashop and enjoy a pot before returning to her bed. Maybe she'd even drink chamomile or mint, so the tea wouldn't keep her alert. She'd have a nap when she returned, make herself get up and work, and then go to bed at her usual time.

The walk through the village was quiet enough. A few people called hello and went about their way. Georgette watched them go and wondered if she'd miss any of them.

Would she miss Mrs. Wilkes? Georgette had always

liked the doctor's wife well enough. And she'd always admired Harriet Lawrence's grace in her lot. Georgette enjoyed the quirk of the baker who scolded her customers, and the way Dr. Wilkes listened to every old woman's woes. She liked the way the creek rolled right through the two hills outside of town and made her think of the Olympic gods come to visit this common village.

"It's true enough," Georgette told herself, "that many a village in England is going to have a quirky proprietress. Maybe it wouldn't be so bad to start again. Somewhere where everyone didn't know I had stuttered for so long."

"Miss Marsh," a voice called.

Georgette turned and found Harriet Lawrence standing nearby. "I wonder if I might have a few minutes of your time."

Georgette smiled at her, hoping the sweet adjective would be used once again for her after being found talking to herself in the street. Otherwise, the adjective just might be 'mad.'

"I was just going to have tea," Georgette told Mrs. Lawrence. "Would you like to join me?"

Harriet nodded, and they stepped into the teashop. Mrs. Yancey nodded at them and offered the table near the window where the morning light was coming into the room. They both ordered scones and jam and tea. Mrs. Yancey talked Georgette into trying a raspberry lavender tea, and Harriet stuck with the Lapsang Souchong.

"I was wondering," Harriet said carefully, "if you saw what happened to the letter I was reading?"

Georgette hadn't expected the question. "I—" She frowned, thinking back. "I folded it up and put in the envelope."

"I remember that too," Harriet said. "I just don't recall what happened next."

"I don't remember. Perhaps I put it in my pocket? Or did I give it to you? Did I drop it while we were talking?"

Harriet frowned, playing with her fingernails. "I looked along the path and where I was sitting and didn't see it."

"I'm so sorry, Mrs. Lawrence," Georgette said. "I will search for it as soon as I return home. If I have it, I will bring it to you."

"Please." Her mouth twisted. "Please. Don't read it."

Georgette reached out. "Of course, I won't, Mrs. Lawrence."

The woman fixed her gaze on Georgette. "I feel we should have long since been closer friends than this, Miss Marsh. May I call you Georgette? Will you be my friend, Georgette?"

She agreed, but there was the rather unkind part of her heart that noted she'd ached for a friend these long years and Mrs. Lawrence had overlooked Georgette time and again. It wasn't so much that Georgette was carrying a grudge—she wasn't. She just didn't have all that much faith in the offer. Perhaps she was just past waiting for Harriet—and everyone else—to notice her. Now that she was playing with the idea of leaving Bard's Crook, someone was offering friendship. The irony wasn't lost on Georgette.

She glanced around the teashop, noting that Miss Schmitz was sitting in the corner, watching the room. Mrs. Thornton, her daughter, and both sons were sitting at the larger table along the wall. The vicar's wife was sitting with two of the village's elderly widows and Virginia Baker of all people. Even Miss Hallowton was standing near the window, picking up a package. Mrs. Hanover from the day before had arrived once again, and she was sitting with a solitary pot of tea and some parcels on the chair opposite her.

Georgette glanced back at Harriet, who seemed to be lost in her own gaze as it wandered around the room. "Tell me, Georgette. What kind of things do you enjoy doing?"

"I like to read books," Georgette said carefully.

"Do you? Have you read the newest Joseph Jones book about our dysfunctional little hamlet?"

Georgette bit her bottom lip, avoiding Harriet's gaze to avoid sharing the sudden rush of humor. "I have." Georgette cleared her throat as Mrs. Yancey returned and then carefully accepted her pot of tea and plate of scones.

"I haven't read it yet," Harriet confessed. "At the end of the last one, I was a woman nearly but not quite abandoned. I haven't even dared to ask what happened to my husband."

"He died in an auto accident," Georgette told Harriet, trying to channel that gentleness that Charles Aaron had shown her.

Harriet nodded, shuddering. "I suppose even this Joseph Jones would have seen it in poor taste to keep him in there."

Georgette winced, nibbling on her bottom lip.

"And me?" Harriet asked. "What happened to me?"

"Your character wasn't there as much. The author wrote more about people who don't match up to our villagers. It's more…ah…imaginative this time."

Harriet's gaze focused on Georgette's face. Georgette almost felt as though the woman's gaze sharpened, and internally Georgette was wincing. "When we spoke about the first book, you said you didn't think there was a connection between the book and our village."

Georgette glanced down at her plate, her lips twitching. She had forgotten that. For a moment, she panicked and then she glanced up and shrugged. "Mrs. Baker prefers me a little dim. I didn't want to disappoint her."

Harriet's gaze widened and darted to Mrs. Baker, and then she placed her hand over her lips to muffle the sudden shout of laughter. "She does. Oh my goodness, Georgette, you are wicked. I had no idea."

Georgette's smile was as wicked as Harriet's claim when she added, "Not so sweet, then?"

Harriet paused before she offered, "Maybe a bit nuanced."

Georgette grinned at her, widely and openly. Then she glanced to the side and noted that Miss Schmitz had slid down in her chair. Before she could react, Miss Thornton screamed.

Dear heavens, Georgette thought, Miss Schmitz looks dead!

10

GEORGETTE DOROTHY MARSH

Georgette stood in a rush and hurried across the teashop. She placed her hand on Miss Schmitz's chest and noticed that she was breathing. "We need Dr. Wilkes," she told Harriet. "She's alive."

Georgette unbuttoned the two buttons at the woman's neck to help make sure Miss Schmitz was breathing as easily as possible. Georgette thought Miss Schmitz was at least somewhat aware. Slowly, the woman opened her eyes. There was a look of utter agony in them. She didn't speak, but she slowly took hold of her jaw. Georgette would have thought that she only had a bad toothache if not for that pain-filled gaze and the fact that she wasn't speaking.

"It's probably another of her games." Mrs. Yancey moved the small, round table out of Georgette's way and helped as Georgette lowered the woman to the ground, laying her carefully out.

"Perhaps," Georgette replied quietly, but with a fierce glance she added, "but what if this isn't a game and we did nothing?"

Mrs. Yancey winced as she stood up. "Mrs. Lawrence went for the doctor. I'll shoo everyone out. If she's really ill, she doesn't need an audience. If she isn't, well—she doesn't deserve their help, does she?"

Georgette nodded. She took hold of Miss Schmitz's hand. "Help is coming. You're not alone."

A tear slipped from Miss Schmitz's eye, and Georgette gently rubbed the back of her hand. The door to the teashop was ringing as people stepped from the shop, so she didn't notice when someone dropped to their knees next to her.

"Are you all right, Georgette?"

She glanced up and saw Detective Aaron and Charles. Charles was next to her while Detective Aaron crouched down by Miss Schmitz's head. He was feeling for her pulse as Georgette stared blankly at the two men.

Beyond the Aaron men, the last few patrons were leaving with their gazes fixed on Georgette kneeling next to the woman. Mrs. Baker took in the scene with callous interest, Miss Hallowton had her hand to her mouth and looked sick, Mrs. Thornton was saying something to her children and had her daughter tucked into her shoulder.

Georgette heard her name called a time or two before she jerked back to the Aaron men. "I...she just slumped over. It was very sudden. I thought she might be dead."

"Someone went for the doctor?" Detective Aaron asked.

She nodded. "I was having tea with Mrs. Lawrence when I saw that Miss Schmitz had collapsed. At about the same time, Miss Thornton noticed and started screaming." Georgette continued to hold Miss Schmitz's hand as another tear slipped down the woman's cheek.

"Perhaps a heart attack?" Charles asked Joseph.

"She would be able to speak if she were having a heart attack," Joseph replied.

"Her mouth hurts," Georgette told them. "Or perhaps her jaw. She is in quite a lot of pain, I think."

"Should we take her to the doctor's house?" Charles asked. He looked at the door. "What is taking the man so long?"

Georgette let them worry about it while she hummed to Miss Schmitz, trying to make her feel better. She noted that the woman's muscles were quite tight and seemed to be winding even tighter. It was almost as though every muscle and bone in her hand had turned to a trembling stone. She was gasping as her limbs remained tense as boards. "It will be all right, Miss Schmitz. We'll get the doctor here and he'll help you feel better. Go ahead and rest, and I'll look after you."

Miss Schmitz let her eyes close and sighed even though she didn't relax at all. Charles placed his hand on Georgette's back as if willing some of his strength into her.

They were waiting like that when Dr. Wilkes came running up. He asked several questions as he examined Miss Schmitz while Mrs. Yancey looked on.

"Has she been spasming like this for a while?"

Georgette nodded. "She seems to be in quite a lot of pain," she repeated. "Her breathing has been difficult, but I'm not sure if that's the pain or if she's not getting enough air." Georgette smoothed the prone woman's hair.

"Gentle with her, Miss Marsh," Dr. Wilkes said. "Like

you said, she's in rather a lot of pain. I'll get my auto, and we'll move her to my surgery."

"I'll stay with her."

Dr. Wilkes's brows lifted, but he didn't object. "She doesn't seem to have anyone else. Perhaps the detective can discover that for us. If she has family, they'll want to come." The way he said it made it clear that he didn't think Miss Schmitz would survive.

"What's the matter with her?" Georgette asked, taking the doctor's hand before he could leave.

"If I'm not very much mistaken, I believe she's been poisoned. I saw her recently. Listened to her heart and her lungs. She was strong as an ox, and I told her I thought she'd outlive us all. Now look at her. She might linger on, but I don't think she's going to come out of this well. Or at all."

Miss Schmitz still had her eyes closed, and Georgette didn't think she'd heard her prognosis. Perhaps that was a small mercy.

"Poisoned?" Detective Aaron asked. He stood suddenly. "How long ago?"

"An hour? A half-hour? It depends on how much she was given. I need to care for her, however. I'll leave this to you. Miss Marsh, stay with her. I'll be back in a moment. We'll do what we can to make her comfortable."

Georgette remained as Dr. Wilkes left. He returned with a stretcher, and he and Charles moved Miss Schmitz onto it while Georgette arranged her dress to preserve Miss Schmitz's modesty. She wasn't sure if Miss Schmitz was aware at the moment, but Georgette felt strongly that they should do whatever was possible to ease her.

Georgette hurried ahead and opened the teashop door

while Charles and Dr. Wilkes carried her out. The auto was outside the door, and the door was opened, so they could slide her into the seat, producing a low moan from Miss Schmitz as they did so. Another tear escaped Miss Schmitz, who whispered as Georgette twisted her body to sit behind the seat on the floor of the auto. "Help me."

Georgette took Miss Schmitz's hand again. "We're trying, Miss Schmitz. Can you take a deep breath?"

It was the wrong thing to say. She gasped horribly as she tried and then coughed. Georgette cried with Miss Schmitz as they motored through the village towards the doctor's home and surgery. Of all the terrible things to witness.

"Are you all right, Georgette?" Charles asked softly.

"I'll be fine." She sniffed and found his handkerchief was near her cheek. She took it but used it to wipe away Miss Schmitz's tears.

They arrived a few moments later, and Georgette let Charles pull her from the floor of the auto. Her legs had become a bit numb on the ride over, and she needed him to hold her up while the feeling recovered but insisted he help Dr. Wilkes when the doctor was ready to move the stretcher.

Poor Miss Schmitz moaned again as they moved her. Georgette cried along with the woman and followed as the gents carried her inside.

"Georgette," Charles said, taking her hand. "Maybe you shouldn't…"

"Stay with her while she dies?" Georgette finished. She smiled, feeling as though she were channeling his gentleness. "I won't rest easy for the remainder of my life if I were to leave her alone."

She found Miss Schmitz lying on the bed in the surgery and sat nearby. "May I mop her face? Maybe rub her feet?"

Dr. Wilkes nodded. "She's clearly in pain. If I give her morphine, I'm afraid it will kill her."

Georgette ignored him. She wasn't going to advise him on what to do, obviously. She was sure he didn't actually want her comments. He was simply speaking aloud and as usual, she wasn't someone people recognized as being present.

"There must be something you can do to help her." Charles's voice carried from the doorway, and Georgette bit her bottom lip as she realized that Dr. Wilkes was speaking to Charles.

"I suspect that anything I do will kill her."

"Would that be wrong?" Charles asked. Georgette looked up in shock and met his gaze. "I don't mean that how it sounded. She's just so miserable."

"Perhaps," Georgette snapped, "you can take this conversation outside."

She crossed to the bath as they stepped outside the room and filled a pitcher, then poured that water into the waiting dish by the bedside. Wetting the wash cloth, Georgette mopped Miss Schmitz's forehead and realized she'd slipped out of awareness. Georgette check her to ensure she was breathing before going to the door to tell Dr. Wilkes.

"It might be kinder to leave her to my wife, Miss Marsh," he told Georgette, "and see if you can discover if she has family to call. If there is someone who needs to see her, now is the time."

Georgette hesitated but thought the doctor was right. Detective Aaron was a good man, but he might not be the best to explain to family what had happened. "Mr. Aaron? Would you come with me?"

He answered by holding out his arm for her.

"Poison?" Georgette immediately asked after they were outside. "Poison? Why would anyone do such a thing?" Charles had that gentle look on his face again. "All right. I suppose I know why, but who could have a secret worth killing over?"

"What would you do, I wonder, if she actually knew your secret?"

Georgette stared at him. "Are you insinuating that I poisoned her?"

"Of course I'm not." Charles took her hand and set it on his elbow. "I'm only saying that I have little doubt that you're not the only one with a life-altering secret in this...this..."

"Dysfunctional little hamlet?" Georgette supplied. She started to smile and then felt guilty for it.

"Just so."

11

CHARLES AARON

The house that Miss Schmitz lived in was tiny. Smaller even than Georgette's little cottage. It did, however, have a lovely patch of flowers outside and a cat sitting in the window. Georgette clucked to the cat as she approached the door. It was like her, he thought, to notice the details and to take in account the feelings of even a cat. He doubted anyone went unnoticed when Georgette was around.

"Does she live alone?" Charles asked her. She glanced up with those honey-brown eyes, and they were shining more than they should have been. "Don't think about it," he said. "We'll do what we can for her."

"Perhaps I shouldn't have left." Georgette looked fraught with concern. "I told her I wouldn't leave her alone and then I did."

"If she has a loved one, my dear Georgie, she wants

them there. Even over you, as comforting as I'm sure you are to her."

Georgette knocked on the door and there wasn't an answer. The cat placed a paw against the window. "Do you think it's very bad if we let ourselves into her house?"

"She's dying, Georgette. If she lives alone, she can't give you permission. If she does not, anyone reasonable would understand. Joseph certainly will. I'm sure he's investigating that teashop carefully trying to identify where the poison came from, though, so he can't give us official permission, but he will after the fact."

Georgette shuddered. "Maybe the poisoning was a random act."

Charles's doubt-filled glance met her own. "You don't think so, and neither do I."

She shook her head and knocked again. A moment later, she seemed to steel herself before she opened the door to the cottage. It wasn't locked and she stepped inside with Charles only a step after her. It was small enough to all be one floor with what looked like a parlor, kitchen, bath, and bedroom. There was a small ladder that led up to a loft.

Georgette peered into the parlor then stepped into the bedroom, finding a desk. "I'll look through her desk for letters or perhaps an address book."

Charles looked around the tiny bedroom again. It was too small for them to not trip over each other, and Charles suspected his lovely Georgette wasn't quite comfortable with such close quarters while they were secluded. He left her to the bedroom and went to the kitchen. There was a box with bread and a bowl with onions and potatoes.

There were a few letters on the small table, and he looked them over, but they were only a few things from the grocer and the post office. Nothing that provided further information on who Miss Schmitz was or who her people were. Charles returned to the small hall area and pulled down the ladder.

Likely, he thought as he climbed the steps, that it was only a storage area. As his head rose above the floor and into the loft, however, he noted the small bed. Perhaps Miss Schmitz didn't live alone? He heard a sound and paused, but it was only Georgette talking to the cat. He smiled at the idea and realized if he could persuade her to love him, he'd hear her talking to her dogs often.

She wouldn't, he thought, be very happy in London for long. They'd need to find another place to live. Perhaps, they could reveal that Georgette Marsh—no, Georgette Aaron—was the author, Joseph Jones.

Perhaps with the release of her new series Josephine Marie. Or perhaps she'd be happier to release Josephine Marie under her own name while leaving those early books in Joseph Jones's name? No, he thought, they'd have to rebuild a career around the new author name.

Those weren't the thoughts he should be pursing at that moment. He stopped listening to Georgette talk to the cat and stepped out into the small loft. The room didn't allow him to stand upright. He was so focused on the desk next to the bed, it took him a moment to take in the full view. Tiny bed—more of a cot really. The tiny desk. A small trunk with a few hooks for dresses on the wall. And reaching from behind the cot—a hand.

Charles stared for a moment, trying to make sense of it, then cursed and hurried across the floor to drop to his knees.

The body was an older woman. She was breathing

quietly, but her limbs were stiff. He cursed again and lifted her from the floor to the cot. Her eyes went wide and he said to her, "Don't be afraid."

That statement did nothing to calm her, so he guessed what Georgette would say and added, "I'm here with my friend. I will send her to you and get you help."

The woman nodded. She wasn't quite as stiff as Miss Schmitz had been and she groaned, "Thank you."

He knew he needed to hurry for the doctor in case anything could be done for her, but he asked, "Did you eat anything that Miss Schmitz also ate?"

The woman groaned again. "Chocolates. Shouldn't have."

"You really shouldn't have," Charles said. "Miss Schmitz is also ill." He stood as tall as he could and called, "Georgette! There's a woman here. She needs you while I get the doctor."

He heard her gasp, the clatter of her rushing to the ladder and then he stopped her. "Let me down first, please. I'm afraid it's even tighter up here than down there."

"Is she—?"

"She's not quite so bad, I think," he said as he quickly descended. "She can talk. Keep her calm. Maybe don't explain what is happening."

Georgette's eyes swam with tears, but she nodded quickly. As he was rushing out the door, Georgette was moving into the kitchen. He had little doubt that some thought had occurred to her that would bring the poor old woman relief.

Charles ran through the village, passing his nephew, and stopped long enough to say, "A serving woman who lives with Miss Schmitz is also ill. She said they both ate chocolates." With quick directions, Charles sent Joseph to Georgette and hurried on for the doctor.

※

GEORGETTE DOROTHY MARSH

Georgette was well and truly afraid that she was going to be holding this woman's hand and dabbing her forehead with a wet cloth while she died in the cottage. The woman wouldn't be her first body. She'd buried her grandmother as a little girl and her parents when she was barely eighteen years old. Even still, she'd never had to do it alone.

"I'm Georgette," she said after too long. "I'm afraid I was there when Miss Schmitz fell ill. We came here to look for names of her family."

The woman groaned. "My arms and legs. My jaw."

Georgette met her gaze. "Perhaps I might try rubbing them?"

She grunted a yes, and Georgette carefully massaged the woman's arms. She was still and her muscles were spasming, but moving them seemed to provide a little relief. Maybe it wasn't so much lesser pain but the fact that each touch made her fully aware that she wasn't alone. It must have been terrible to have the poison hit her while she was without anyone nearby to help, leaving her waiting in fear and pain for Miss Schmitz to return.

Georgette began talking to the woman as she worked, randomly speaking about the weather, the teashop, the new tea flavors she'd been trying. She chattered until the door opened and Detective Aaron called, "Georgette?"

"Up here," she answered and then told the woman,

"That's Detective Aaron. He'll help us until the doctor gets here."

"Doing fine," the woman groaned and shifted. "This is horrible. Someone poisoned Miss Schmitz? Shouldn't've eaten. Stingy."

Georgette smoothed her hair back as Joseph climbed to the loft.

"Is she—?" His gaze was fixed on where Georgette knelt next to the woman on the cot.

"She's not as bad," Georgette told him. "Did you just eat a little?"

The woman nodded. "One. Chocolates."

Joseph's gaze brightened. "The doctor is coming, and we'll help get her down the ladder with his stretcher. I think we'll need to be quite clever about it."

"We're all right," Georgette replied, using the wash cloth to cool the woman's forehead. "She's breathing easier than Miss Schmitz. Though stiff, she's quite a bit less rigid. She's hot, but the cloth is helping her cool down."

"Keep taking such good care of her, Georgette," Joseph said.

He disappeared down the ladder, and Georgette went back to massaging the woman's limbs, cooling her forehead, and chattering about nothing to distract the woman. After a time, Georgette asked, "What is your name?"

"Ruth Dogger."

Georgette kept talking about random Ruths that she had known over the course of her life. She laughed at herself. "I'm sorry. I don't really know what I'm doing."

"Distracting me," Ruth replied. "Nice. Hurts."

Georgette re-wet the cloth and continued to work until she heard the sound of an auto. It took only minutes for Dr.

Wilkes and Charles to appear. They'd brought with them the local police constable, and the four men, with Joseph, got Ruth out of the loft with Georgette following. She found herself crouched behind the seats on the floor of the auto once again, moving with a woman to the surgery.

Charles pulled Georgette free, but she didn't need to help this time. She followed them in and found Mrs. Wilkes and one of the maids sitting with Miss Schmitz.

"Is she sleeping?"

"Something a little more than normal sleep, he thinks," Mrs. Wilkes replied for her husband, who was attending Ruth Dogger. "The doctor fears that Miss Schmitz won't wake again. What about the other woman?"

Georgette shook her head, sitting down by Miss Schmitz. "I believe she took less of the poison. She seems quite a bit better than Miss Schmitz. Not quite so hot, responding to the washcloths. She's able to speak even though she's quite clearly in pain."

Mrs. Wilkes glanced Georgette over and said rather suddenly, "I'm surprised you were so forward with helping. You're usually so quiet."

Georgette snorted to herself but her voice was kind enough. "Someone had to help. I fear Miss Schmitz has made a number of enemies."

"But not you?" Mrs. Wilkes asked.

Georgette had no intention of answering that. It would open her to follow-up questions that Georgette had no desire to explain. Georgette simply smiled vaguely and found that—once again—putting on her old persona didn't quite fit. The thought to leave Bard's Crook occurred to her once again.

After holding two poisoned women's hands and having

to face that one, at the least, would die, Georgette wondered what this village would do to her if her secrets were uncovered. Even if they'd never found out her secret, she kept slipping back into this vague, dim, simpleton version of herself. It was what people expected of her, and Georgette found that having gone back to it after her first book had been the easiest, but she'd been far less comfortable in that old persona lately. Perhaps she should at least consider the possibility of leaving Bard's Crook.

12

CHARLES AARON

They had to persuade Georgette to leave Ruth Dogger and Miss Schmitz. It was only when Dr. Wilkes told Georgette flatly that Miss Schmitz wouldn't wake again and that Mrs. Dogger was sleeping comfortably and would likely survive that they were able to shoo her out of the doctor's surgery. The walk back to Georgette's cottage was completely silent. He didn't know how to comfort her.

"We need to find the poisoner," Georgette announced. "We can't let this stand."

"Joseph will do that, my dear Georgette," Charles said.

She gave him a withering glance, and Charles gaped at the change in her. "I can't...I won't... stand by and do nothing."

"This is his position, Georgette," Charles tried again,

ensuring that he used the gentlest tone he could provide. "If we meddle, we may well ruin his investigation."

Georgette didn't reply, but Charles couldn't help but note that she was moving along at a smart clip once again. Her skirt was snapping against her lovely calves, and her hands were fisted at her sides. He hadn't changed her mind in the slightest.

Charles followed in her wake and when they reached her cottage, she told him, "Detective Aaron, even the constable, they can't do for those women what I can."

Her dogs were barking at the other side of the door, which opened a moment later to reveal Marian and four of the young dogs, who darted out to Georgette and sat down with wagging tails.

"What can you do?" he asked sincerely.

"You'll never get the women of this village to reveal to you why they were being targeted by Miss Schmitz. Never. But I could."

He stared at her, taking in her cheeks flushed with anger, her shining honey-brown eyes, the way her perfect white teeth nibbled on her bottom lip, and then conjured that gentle side of himself. "But Georgette, they don't confide in you now. Why would they confide their secrets to a person they don't bother to see?"

"I'll make them," she said. "Marian, you'll help. We need paper, Eunice, and tea." She shot a glance back at Charles. "I fear I cannot offer you tea today, Mr. Aaron."

To his utter shock, she nodded at him once again and shut the door in his face. Charles blinked at the door before turning away. He walked, bemused, back to the little house where he and his nephew had been forced to rent a shared room and took his satchel, leaving the house for the library.

Perhaps Miss Hallowton might offer him a place to work in her library.

Charles stopped in the pub on the way and found Harrison Parker sitting at the bar. He considered taking a table and then sighed and crossed to the younger man. He tried not to scowl at the broader shoulders or handsomer jaw when he took the stool next to the man. He ordered fish, chips, and a pint and then turned to Parker. "Why are you here, Parker? In Bard's Crook?"

Parker glanced over and then blushed. "My cousin, of course."

"For friendship or marriage?" Charles demanded, ignoring manners.

"Ah, friendship. Marian's like a sister to me. Her father asked me to keep an eye on her."

"So you're avoiding work to follow her around?"

Harrison shot Charles a look. "I don't quite need as much time to get my work done as they think. I double up some days, work a few more hours, and then come here."

"For Miss Marsh?"

Harrison's jaw dropped. He shook his head emphatically. "Marian swears Miss Marsh is an excellent writer and I'd thought to get her to look my stories over, but honestly man, I can't see it. That quiet mouse?"

Charles ignored the rush of relief. In a jovial tone, he said, "I know some fellows in publishing. Tell me about these stories of yours."

GEORGETTE DOROTHY MARSH

"The people in the teashop don't necessarily matter," Georgette told Marian, "given that Mrs. Dogger was poisoned as well. Who matters isn't who was in the teashop but who gave her chocolates that were laced with, well, whatever they used."

Eunice set a tray of sandwiches on the table, followed with a teapot. "If I were to guess, Mrs. Yancey doesn't want anyone to know if—" The dogs' barking drowned out whatever Eunice was going to say, and they all looked towards the door. Eunice rose and walked down the hall to the front door as someone knocked.

"Who do you think it is?" Marian whispered.

"Your great aunt or one of the Aaron men," Georgette whispered back. "No one else ever comes here."

Eunice walked back to the kitchen. "It's Harriet Lawrence. She wants to know if you're quite all right."

Georgette's jaw dropped, and her gaze darted to Marian, who jumped up. "Ooh! Maybe she has an idea of what has been happening with Miss Schmitz."

Georgette followed Marian to the parlor after asking Eunice to bring tea. Harriet turned from where she was looking out the window and took in the two women. "I shouldn't have simply dropped in, but I was worried about you. Are you quite all right?"

Georgette provided her usual vague answers as they sat, but Harriet Lawrence's gaze narrowed as Marian twitched suddenly and stood. She crossed to the small desk where Georgette had left much of her book work out and closed the roll-top. It was too overt not to notice, and Georgette winced. It would have been quite better for Marian to leave it be.

"Would you like some tea?" Georgette asked as Eunice arrived with the tea tray. She poured a cup quickly, offering a few of the small sandwiches, and Harriet took the plate with a focused gaze. Georgette sighed. She suspected that her first local was beginning to realize that she had been hiding who she really was. Rather than give herself away, Georgette tried for a vague smile and stared beyond Harriet's shoulder.

"Is Miss Schmitz going to be all right?" Harriet asked.

Georgette paused, thinking that Harriet and the doctor's wife were rather close friends. Why was the woman coming to ask Georgette when her closest friend would certainly have access to better details and be more inclined to share? That being said, however, Georgette didn't think it was wise to pretend stupidity about something that it was known that she knew.

"The doctor seems to think that Miss Schmitz will not wake."

Harriet's mouth dropped open for a moment and then her state seemed to occur to her and she snapped her mouth closed. "What happened?"

Again, Georgette wasn't quite sure how to answer. Harriet was far better connected to the gossip of the village and why someone might try to kill Miss Schmitz.

"Both Miss Schmitz and her rather unfortunate—well, I don't know if Ruth Dogger is a servant or a relative or what, but they were both victims of a poisoning."

Harriet set her teacup down. "Would you repeat that?"

Georgette said it all again and Harriet stared.

"Do you know why?"

The demand was so intense that Georgette was instantly sure that Harriet had a very specific reason for wanting to know that had little to do with Miss Schmitz and everything to do with Harriet Lawrence.

"I assume it has something to do with how she was trying to uncover who had secrets and how to discover them."

"How do you know that?" Harriet asked.

Georgette glanced at Marian and then, with a tilted head and examining gaze, Georgette replied, "She tried to get me to reveal what my secrets were."

Harriet paused for a moment, eyes narrowed. "You don't have secrets, Georgette. What an odd little woman Miss Schmitz is to focus on you when there are those of us who actually have things to hide. It must be nice for you."

"Why?" Marian asked as she handed her teacup to Georgette to refill. "What is nice for Georgette?"

"To have a simple life without secrets. A pure life, really."

Georgette blinked rapidly into her teacup and then sipped it before she attempted to reply. Of all the cheek, she thought. To look at Georgette's life and the cage that Bard's Crook had put her in as a pure life?

"Surely we all have something we would do differently," Marian asked. There was something in her tone that had Georgette turning to stare at her friend. "You, perhaps? Is that why you said that?"

Georgette glanced back at Harriet and knew immediately that Harriet did have something to hide. The startled, horrified look in her gaze was answer enough, and Georgette remembered how she had found Harriet weeping over a letter. A letter lost afterwards.

"Did she find your secrets out?" Georgette asked carefully in a sweet tone that one would assume wasn't prying.

Harriet's hands were shaking when she tried to mask her concerns with her teacup. The cup rattled against the saucer and she hastily set it down, trying for a smile and failing into something more like a grimace.

"She did, didn't she?" Georgette said, certain. "She found out something about you."

Harriet's lips quivered. "I suppose she must've. I received a letter in the mail demanding money or my secret would be revealed. I didn't think anyone knew." She sighed heavily. "My husband had an idea. He wrote a book with quite a tirade on unrighteous women and dedicated it to me, you know. His little revenge along with all of the petty day-to-day things he did." She sniffed and pressed away a tear with her ring finger. "He didn't even know he had it right. If he had—my goodness, he'd have made it a special mission to make me suffer."

"Those days are over," Georgette told Harriet kindly. "Chin up."

"The threats are over as well, I imagine," Marian said. "As someone discovered who was behind your letter and killed them."

"You are assuming that Miss Schmitz sent the letter," Georgette told her.

"Who else could it have been?"

Georgette stood and paced as she considered. Harriet seemed grateful for a distracted Georgette. Perhaps Mrs. Lawrence expected for Georgette and Marian to demand an explanation of what Miss Schmitz knew about Harriet, but Georgette didn't want to know.

She considered who she'd seen acting oddly around Miss

Schmitz. Mrs. Yancey, Mrs. Hanover, Jasper Thornton. Georgette, herself, she realized with a little smile. Her own situation showed Georgette just how little acting odd around the woman mattered for motive to kill. She sighed as she paced, considering Harriet. If someone had asked Georgette who might have engineered Miss Schmitz's impending death, Georgette wouldn't have even guessed that Harriet Lawrence would have a reason for a grudge.

Georgette looked at Marian. They needed to track down Detective Aaron and ensure he knew that Miss Schmitz had possibly been playing a dangerous game. She recalled what she'd seen at Miss Schmitz's home. It had been small, cramped, and quite poor. The food, what little there was, had been sparse and cheap. Georgette had seen the bowl of potatoes and onions and had little doubt that Miss Schmitz and Mrs. Dogger had been eating as poorly as Georgette had before the success of her book.

"Did you pay?"

Harriet's mouth twisted as she nodded. "Rather more than I'd like to admit."

13

CHARLES AARON

"I don't like any part of this," Charles said.

Joseph was going through Miss Schmitz's cottage. He'd gathered up the paperwork and letters and put them in his satchel, and he'd carefully gathered the chocolates and sent them off with the constable. They needed to discover just what Miss Schmitz and Mrs. Dogger had been poisoned with. Dr. Wilkes was betting that the poison was strychnine, but they needed to be entirely sure.

"Why would you like it?" Joseph asked. "This is a mess of notable proportions. Quiet little village, little old maid being struck down for doing what lonely old women do. You know, the last murder case I worked was here in Bard's Crook. Since then I've worked all kinds of crimes, but not a murder. How is it that this pleasant little village is more dangerous than a city as large as London?"

Charles paced in the tiny hall while Joseph examined the

cottage, looking for anything out of the way. "If some meddling little woman like this Laurieann Schmitz was in danger, what would happen to Georgette? If these people knew?"

"We need to get Georgette and Marian out of here," Joseph told Charles as he found a notebook and shoved it in his satchel. "It would be nice if we could get more than a scrap of their time."

Charles laughed. "I out and out asked that bloke, Parker, what his intentions were towards Georgette. Do you know that I could ask a half-dozen women to marry me in London and be assured of a positive response? What have I come to?"

Joseph shot his uncle a mocking look. "If you want to be bored, you could marry one of those women. You'd end up with two sons, one daughter, a pot belly, and a woman who has gone to fat and is still boring."

Charles didn't dignify his nephew with a response.

Joseph, however, paused in looking through the little house. "Are Parker's intentions towards Marian?" Joseph asked, bypassing Charles's potential worry. "Bloody hell, we sound like a couple of clucking hens."

Charles snorted as Joseph locked up the cottage, and they walked towards the constables' offices. Joseph intended to go through the paperwork and see if he could narrow down what Miss Schmitz had been up to while Charles was going to try, once again, to garner Georgette's attention.

"Detective Aaron," Marian called as they turned onto the street where the offices were located. "We have been looking for you."

The two men turned and found the dual objects of their affections walking arm in arm with their dogs surrounding them like a barking windstorm. Georgette was slim in one of her newer dresses. Charles didn't think he'd seen this one before. It was peach with a large white collar and reached her mid-calves. Her brown hair glinted with gold streaks in the sunlight.

"If we're successful," Charles told his nephew in an undertone, "this is the view we would become accustomed to."

"I'd be happy to grow so accustomed."

"They'd be happier if they found themselves neighbors in whatever village I find for Georgette and myself."

"You find?" Joseph laughed aloud but kept his words quiet. "You have a woman discovering that her wants and choices matter. She's going to have a rather vociferous vote, I bet. She'll find this village, and you'll find yourself merely hoping for a good pub."

Charles chuckled and then said in a nearly undetectable voice, "At least Georgette would listen to me to some degree. Your Marian will choose wherever Georgette lives, and you'll be entirely without a voice at all."

"Or they'll choose together without regard to either of us, and we'll be chasing after them rather like we are at the moment."

"Gentlemen," Georgette said pleasantly, ignoring their whispering. "We've come across a rather surprising bit of information."

"Have you?" Charles asked. "I find that I am entirely unsurprised. You did, after all, warn me you would."

Georgette smiled at him, just a little, and he breathed a sigh of relief. He didn't want her in danger, but he also didn't want her upset with him. He didn't think that anyone would discover her secrets if she were careful, and he had to admit she'd kept her secrets rather well for far longer than he'd been involved.

"We think," Marian said almost triumphantly, "that Miss Schmitz was blackmailing some of our fellow Bard's Crookers."

Joseph choked. "Surely not."

Georgette simply lifted a brow at him while Marian shot back, "You heard how she treated Georgie. If Miss Schmitz operated so aggressively with others who aren't as kind as Georgette, well—clearly someone poisoned the woman."

Georgette hesitated and then admitted. "I had been thinking she was acting so odd that it would make a perfect blackmail plot. I was considering it for my next book about Harper's Bend." The last two words were whispered. Georgette leaned down to scratch her favorite dog's ears. "Miss Schmitz was certainly a foolish woman, but even foolish women act as they do for a reason. Money is always a compelling reason, and really, it's not like poor Miss Schmitz could easily support herself in other ways."

Marian scowled and then she sighed. "Truthfully, they put our sex on a pedestal, Georgette. They're thinking that no good woman would behave in such a manner."

Georgette smiled wickedly, winking at Marian. "No good woman, but perhaps a bad and greedy one."

"It would have been a very ham-handed blackmail plot," Charles said. "If you wrote it, Georgette, I'd tell you that it was unbelievable and that blackmailers would be more secretive with their actions. I'd expect better of you."

"Well, yes," Marian laughed, "of Georgette, certainly. But we're considering the desperate actions of a poor, foolish woman."

"What we do know," Georgette told them, "is that one

of our neighbors has said she was being blackmailed. We know that Miss Schmitz certainly acted as though she intended to use any secrets she uncovered and that generally kindly women despise Miss Schmitz. We know that someone blackmailed our neighbor, and it certainly seems likely that, were it Miss Schmitz, whether she was a good blackmailer or a very bad blackmailer—she angered someone to the point where they decided to kill an otherwise harmless old woman."

Joseph cleared his throat. "Nicely and quite accurately summed up, Georgette. You're very right."

"It is a bit mad, though, isn't it?"

"It is," Charles said fervently.

"I can't really see it, either," Georgette admitted. "But the facts sort of lead themselves, don't they? If we find proof that Miss Schmitz was the blackmailer."

"They do indeed," Charles told her. "Perhaps we can help Joseph by discussing who has been acting odd around Miss Schmitz and then narrow down where he should focus next? I know that Joseph could use your help in going through her paperwork, Marian."

Joseph paused at that, given it was out and out a terrible idea and probably against regulation. Better, Charles thought, to have them interfere with Joseph and Charles nearby than off on their own doing who knew what. It was a simple chocolate that was killing Miss Schmitz after all.

"I was thinking of visiting Ruth," Georgette told Charles. "Do you want to visit with me? I haven't felt right about leaving her."

Charles nodded. He did not want to visit the woman. No one was really sure if she was a servant or just another even poorer relative of Miss Schmitz and neither of them had been in the position to be asked. He did, however, want Georgette's attention, and if he had to get it by following her around on her good deeds, then he would.

He held out his arm, and they made their way through the village towards the doctor's house and surgery. Georgette was mostly quiet as they walked and finally he asked her, "Are you all right, my dear Georgette?"

She glanced up at him. "No, not really. I don't think two women should have to die because of the stupid actions of one. I don't think that things should be so hard and that so many should be suffering. Children are going hungry in our country, Charles. Women like Miss Schmitz don't have someone to support them, and the ways of the past aren't any use to them now. What was she supposed to do?"

"Other than blackmail?" He felt his face transforming to gentle again. "Write a book like you did?"

Georgette huffed. "Whether or not I'm as talented as you say—"

"You are."

"Not everyone is. Perhaps I am—"

"You are."

Georgette smacked his forearm, shooting him a glance. "If I wasn't? I'm just as unemployable as she is, Charles. Her life? Her worries? There but for the grace of God, go I. It would have been so easy for her life to be mine." Georgette shook her head. "This is bringing it all back. The worries about supporting myself. The horror when I realized my dividends would not take care of me and Eunice anymore. The realization that there was nothing I could do. Even keeping chickens—and I hate chickens—wouldn't have been enough. Taking in mending? No one pays for that now. The whole of the world is struggling to survive, and with Miss Schmitz and I? There's nothing to recommend us."

Charles paused and pulled Georgette into the shadow of a great oak tree. "You are not Laurieann Schmitz."

"I know I'm not, but—" Georgette shook her head, eyes shining too brightly to be anything other than tears.

Charles cupped her face, tilting her gaze to his when she wouldn't meet his eyes. "It isn't just that you have talent as a writer, Georgette. When you were faced with the same dilemmas as Miss Schmitz, you found another way. It's true that things are harder now than they were a decade ago. It's true that banks have failed, and the whole of the world seems to be going bankrupt and hungry. It's true that for you and for Miss Schmitz things are harder than they are for Marian Parker."

A tear slipped down Georgette's cheek.

"I suppose that the world taught you that you needed someone to save you, to come along and take care of you."

She nodded.

"When that didn't happen, you had choices. You could look for some...some..."

"Mr. Collins," Georgette told him with a watery laugh.

"A Mr. Collins," Charles agreed, instantly understanding her reference to Jane Austen. "Some way out that wouldn't have given you happiness even if it gave you a roof over your head. But you didn't."

"I would have," Georgette admitted.

"Perhaps." Charles very much doubted it. "But when no one came along to save you, what did you do?"

"I saved myself," she said. "I wrote my book."

"I have little doubt that some other publisher would have picked up your book," Charles told her. "But, I also have little doubt that if that plan failed, you'd have found a way to another one and another one and another one, until one stuck. None of those plans would have been blackmail. Sympathize if you must with Miss Schmitz. Empathize with her loneliness or her struggles or how you guess she must have felt as she realized her circumstances had changed as yours had. But, remember, you aren't her."

Georgette's mouth twisted and she stepped away. With her movement, Charles let his hand fall. She took in a deep breath and walked from the shadows under the oak tree back to the lane.

"Have you thought more about leaving Bard's Crook?" Charles asked as they restarted their walk.

14

GEORGETTE DOROTHY MARSH

"Yes, actually," Georgette replied, her voice fading as Mrs. Baker and Miss Hallowton left the doctor's house. Georgette muttered, "Lovely."

She sighed and then ensured her gaze stayed on the ground; trying to find that vague, absentminded expression was becoming more and more difficult. It was these very moments that made her think again of leaving Bard's Crook. Perhaps she'd go visit a few little villages not too far from London.

"Miss Marsh!" Mrs. Baker said with a cutting tone. "You and Mr. Aaron seem to be chummy."

Georgette laughed emptily. "How is Miss Schmitz and Mrs. Dogger?" she asked Miss Hallowton.

"They wouldn't let us see them," Miss Hallowton said sourly. "I don't know why not."

Georgette guessed it was because Mrs. Baker was there

for the gossip and Miss Hallowton was about as comforting as a sharp elbow jabbed in the side.

"Don't bother trying to see them yourself," Mrs. Baker said. Her bright eyes flicked over Charles and Georgette, and then Mrs. Baker purred to Charles, "Tell me, Mr. Aaron, you're visiting from London, yes?"

"Yes," Charles said agreeably. "Lovely to get out of the city."

"But Bard's Crook. Really?"

"My nephew took a liking to it when he was here last." Charles lied so agreeably that Georgette had to hide a snicker.

"Indeed? Now, he's the detective, isn't he?"

Charles nodded.

"What do you do, Mr. Aaron?"

Georgette kept her gaze vacant as though she were bored. Inside, however, she was offended. It wasn't that she expected Mr. Aaron to desire her, but Mrs. Baker could at least throw herself at him when Georgette wasn't holding his elbow.

"I work in an office, Mrs. Baker." There was snap in his voice that had Georgette risking a glance to him before she dulled her face again.

Oh! It was hard pretending to be entirely unaware at moments like these. It had been, she thought, far easier to let her mind write stories when nothing interesting was happening around her. Perhaps she hadn't been pretending all these years so much as she hadn't been any more interested in them than they were in her.

"I do think I should just step inside and see Mrs. Dogger," Georgette said. She let go of Charles's arm and stepped forward, glancing back at him with a smirk. Yes, she would leave him to those two.

Georgette hurried towards the doctor's house, hearing Mrs. Baker say as she went, "I don't know why Miss Marsh expects them to let her in when they wouldn't let us in."

"Ah," Charles cleared his throat and Georgette hid her snicker as she knocked on the door.

The door was opened by one of the women who worked for the doctor. "We're not accepting visitors at this time."

"I'm not here to see you," Georgette said firmly. "I'm here to see Mrs. Dogger."

"The doctor—" the maid began, but Georgette shook her head.

"I fear I must intrude," Georgette replied even more firmly. "I promised Mrs. Dogger I would stay with her and I mean to do so. I found her, you see. And she doesn't have family here, does she?"

Georgette quite boldly stepped past the girl, ignoring her objections, and went into the surgery portion of the house and made her way to Mrs. Dogger's room.

"I thought I said no visitors," Dr. Wilkes said to the maid, but Georgette stepped past him as boldly and went in to Mrs. Dogger.

"Hello, Ruth," Georgette said when the woman cracked her eyes. "Are you feeling any better?"

She nodded just slightly and Georgette went about taking care of the woman, fluffing her pillows and holding a glass of water to her lips.

"I'm sorry I left you. The doctor wanted me to leave, but I have regretted since I did."

"They say Laurieann won't survive," Mrs. Dogger said. She had dark circles under her eyes and her mostly grey hair was pulled back into a messy knot. Georgette felt certain that this was a woman who took pride in doing what she could for her appearance. "She was a stingy thing, but she didn't throw me out. What am I going to do now?"

Georgette reached out a hand and took Mrs. Dogger's. "Do either of you have family?"

Mrs. Dogger shook her head, a tear leaking out of her eye. "We're all that is left. When she dies, I'll be the only one there to bury her."

"I'll be there with you," Georgette told Mrs. Dogger. "Things will work out all right. We'll figure it out."

Mrs. Dogger sniffled again. "Why would you care?"

"I know what it's like to be nearly alone," Georgette said simply. "None of this is your fault, but I'll help if I can. I wonder..."

Mrs. Dogger closed her eyes, but Georgette knew she was listening. No, she decided, she would help the woman first. She adjusted the question. "I wonder if you'd like me to wash your hair."

"Please."

Georgette left Mrs. Dogger and requested what was needed. In minutes Georgette and the maid were helping Mrs. Dogger to undress and wash. It didn't take long with all of them working together, and Georgette was brushing Mrs. Dogger's hair after putting her into one of Mrs. Wilkes's nightgowns and robes.

"Do you feel better now?"

"Tired," Mrs. Dogger said, "but alive."

Georgette braided the grey and brown hair for her and then fluffed the woman's pillows again. As Mrs. Dogger leaned back, Georgette asked, "Is Miss Schmitz your niece?"

"Cousin."

"She was poisoned."

Mrs. Dogger laughed bitterly.

"Why?"

"Ah," Mrs. Dogger shook her head. "I won't pretend that Laurieann wasn't meddling, but you don't kill people for meddling. You snub them."

Georgette looked down at her hands. "Perhaps she wasn't just meddling. She was blackmailing?"

"No," Mrs. Dogger said immediately.

"She told me that she knew my secrets. When I doubted her, she told me that now she knew I had them and she'd find them out."

"I'm sure she did," Mrs. Dogger sighed. She coughed, and Georgette handed the woman her glass of water again, helping her to drink from it.

"You think she was finding out my secrets for some purpose, but not that she was going to attempt to blackmail me?"

Mrs. Dogger laughed. "Do you think they'll let me have tea?"

"I'll ask," Georgette said, stepping out again and finding the maid to request tea for them both. The maid said she'd need to check with the doctor. Georgette returned to the woman and met her gaze from the doorway to the room. "Tell me what's happening, Ruth."

Ruth swallowed. "You have to understand that Laurieann is very silly." Another tear escaped. "She read this book, The Further Adventures of Harper's Bend. Have you heard of it?"

"I have," Georgette said, wincing. "I understand she identified with a character in the book?"

"Supposedly the author based the book off of the village and real people here. Laurieann decided that the author had based that part off of her. She started acting like the character. I told her that the book had to have been written quite a while ago. It takes time for books to be published. We've only lived here for a few months."

Georgette nodded.

"Laurieann didn't want to believe me. She felt like being in the book would somehow make her feel more, I don't know. It was like she felt seen. Do you know what I mean?"

Did she! Georgette only nodded, but she knew exactly what that felt like—not being seen was the entirety of her life until she'd met Charles, Joseph, and Marian.

"So she decided to make it even more valid. She knew, I think, in her heart of hearts, she knew that the author had based nothing on her. She just wanted to be seen. To be part of the village here. If it took her acting like that Caroline Hardport, then that was what she was going to do."

Georgette sat down again, taking Mrs. Dogger's hand. "Caroline Hardport didn't blackmail anyone."

"And neither did Laurieann. When she wasn't lying to herself, Laurieann has always been scrupulously honest. She wouldn't have taken food from someone's mouth like that. She knows what it's like to go hungry. We only have just enough to get by, and that after selling her much larger house and moving to this village. The tiny little cottage. Laurieann didn't want to descend into poverty watched by the neighbors who had always known her and seen the whole fall from prosperity to poverty. At least here, in Bard's Crook, she was always poor."

Ruth turned her head to the window, and Georgette simply sat with her until the tea came and then sat with her while they both waited for her cousin to die. Miss Schmitz hadn't woken since she'd first slipped into sleep. If the rictus on her face was any indication, it was a mercy.

Georgette stayed until Ruth fell asleep and then covered her carefully. The sun had long since set, and Georgette had reached the point of hunger where her head ached and her stomach was knotted. The maid had offered them both something to eat, but Georgette wouldn't eat actual food while Ruth suffered with broth.

Georgette stopped by to check on Laurieann and found one of the Wilkes's staff sitting in the room. "How is she?"

The maid shook her head. "It won't be long now. It's unfortunate she got enough poison to kill her but not enough to kill her quickly."

"A rest before she sleeps," Georgette said, even though they both knew it wasn't true. The mercy was that Miss Schmitz seemed unaware of her suffering. Her breathing was ragged, and Georgette was guessing that sooner or later those struggling lungs would give out. She crossed to Miss Schmitz, smoothed back her hair, and then dropped a kiss on her forehead.

"The poor, foolish woman," Georgette said without explaining herself. She hurried out of the surgery, bypassing the doctor who only nodded. She had no idea what had happened to Charles and was guessing that he was questioned and examined as a possible replacement for Mrs. Baker's dead spouse. The woman was very clearly looking for a replacement, and her standards were also clear to those who were paying attention. No poor but righteous vicar or kind but—well, Georgette smiled to herself. Wealth seemed to be Mrs. Baker's only requirement.

Truthfully, Georgette had little doubt that the day

would arrive that Mrs. Baker found what she desired. She rather thought, however, that Charles wouldn't be the one who succumbed to Mrs. Baker. Regardless of the woman's charms, Charles seemed to respect the literary portraits Georgette had created, and no man wanted a woman whose gaze was fixed on his pocket rather than his heart.

15

CHARLES AARON

The dogs gave her away even before she'd cleared the gate to the garden. Charles had returned to his rented room, gathered his satchel, and gone to Georgette's cottage to spend the day with her when the maid turned him away at the doctor's door. The maid had, at least, admitted that Georgette had 'barreled' her way inside, but the woman refused to give way again.

Joseph and Marian had arrived before Georgette, and Eunice had eventually fed them afternoon tea and then dinner out of sheer mercy.

Charles rose, nodding to the others, and opened the door before Georgette could. "You look pale," he told her, handing her inside as if she needed his help.

"I am rather given over to hunger," she admitted. She said hello to the dogs while Eunice came out of the kitchens, clucking at her.

"Did they feed you?"

Georgette's pale face seemed to answer Eunice.

"Turned it away, didn't you?"

"I couldn't eat in front of Ruth. She can only have broth and tea." Georgette sniffed, allowing herself the freedom of pressing her temple before she admitted, "I should very much like to wash up and have a little something."

Georgette glanced at the others. "Shall we just be on family terms, then? I find I'm too tired to stand on ceremony and manners." She hurried up the stairs, probably knowing that no one would deny her that. If only she could see her way to recognizing that was why they were here. To turn these friendships into a family instead. Charles had realized as she walked away from him that afternoon that Georgette simply didn't see him as a suitor.

It had taken him the walk to her cottage and Eunice's simple speech to realize it wasn't him. It was how Georgette saw herself.

"She gave up thinking of herself as someone to be loved the way you care for her long ago, and way too young," Eunice told him when he complained that Georgette had left him to Mrs. Baker. "You might have realized that Parker doesn't have a chance, but you don't have one either, lad. Not until she realizes why you're here. Don't think once she does, she'll just fall into your arms either. She'll think on it."

"She sees herself as the side character of a book," Charles muttered.

"Charlotte Lucas but worse," Eunice agreed. "Even Mr. Collins noticed Charlotte. No one sees Georgette, at least according to Georgette." Eunice had been making bread at the time and Charles had invited himself into her kitchens for help. Why she'd softened, he didn't know, but he was glad of it.

He'd been considering avenues of convincing Georgette and had come to the rather startling revelation that he might have to out and out tell her. It wasn't very romantic, but if her mind was entirely closed to being someone's lover, he might not have another choice.

Charles had returned to the parlor and his satchel full of manuscripts, letters from the accountant and other authors. He worked the afternoon away on the dullness of the office work and then paused, staring down at his papers. What had Georgette done? She'd made a list of the things she needed for her house and for herself and Eunice. Georgette had been pegging those things off of her list for a while now. He thought, perhaps, he might do the same.

-Convince Georgette I love her.
    -Convince Georgette to marry me.
    -Convince Georgette to find a house for us.

He smiled to himself for a moment. He really was behaving like an old hen, but that didn't stop him from altering the list.

-Find a house with
    . -an office so I can work from home at least half the time
    -an office for Georgette so she can write dozens more books
    -room for children
    -room for too many books and more to come
    -a garden for smoking pipes in

-a village that has an excellent pub

-create a happily ever after?

Charles snorted. If he could convince her to take him seriously, he might just be able to hand her this list and find that while she was crossing things off of her own list, she might cross things off his list as well. Having the idea of a helpmeet was suddenly far more appealing. Somehow he'd shifted from comfortable bachelor to an uncomfortable bachelor who had seen that perhaps, with the right woman, things would be better together than separate.

He grinned to himself as he added:

-convince Georgette to share her troubles

    -convince Georgette to find a village that will work for Joseph and Marian as well

Charles wouldn't even be surprised if Joseph were to leave Scotland Yard for the office of one of those smaller villages. The boy would, of course, be bored out of his mind. Perhaps he should consider writing detective novels on the side. After Bard's Crook, fictional crimes in a small town might just be what they all needed to recover.

Perhaps, Charles laughed to himself, if Joseph were a very bad writer, he'd be a good writing partner for Georgette. Charles could just see the charm of the Harper's Bend books with a touch of a murder investigation. A quiet village with an entirely unexpected crime. It might be just the thing to sell well.

Charles turned back to his work until Joseph and Marian arrived and then listened to what they had learned, which was to say, nothing. There was not a shred of evidence anywhere in the house or the papers that any blackmailing had been occurring.

Georgette came down the stairs. She'd changed into a jumper and another skirt. Her face was shiny and red, having clearly been scrubbed. Her hair had been let out of the clip that held it back, and she was wearing a pair of flat shoes.

"Is it chilly in here?"

It wasn't, but when she shivered, Charles rose and lit the fire for her. The spring day had turned into rain, and she'd walked that last bit home in the wet. She hadn't looked too damp but perhaps she'd caught a chill.

"You found there was no evidence of blackmailing?" Georgette asked as she curled onto the Chesterfield.

"None of that, Miss Georgie," Eunice said, hands on her hips. "The dining room with you, my dear. That's a hunger headache you're fighting."

"I fear my stomach is past the point of a meal, especially sitting with Ruth while Laurieann was dying."

Eunice eyed Georgette and then declared, "I'll bring you some soup and toast."

Georgette pressed her cheeks. "I do feel sick, but I think it's more heart sick than ill. You didn't find proof of Laurieann Schmitz blackmailing anyone, did you?" she repeated.

Joseph shook his head. "How did you know?"

"I talked to Ruth for rather a long time. Laurieann wanted to be Caroline Hardport." Georgette's bitter laugh had Charles wincing. "The problem is, of course, that someone else is blackmailing people in Bard's Crook. If you were being blackmailed and you were challenged by a Caroline Hardport-want-to-be, who would you think was blackmailing you? Some friend who knew your secrets or the stranger who'd come to town and was acting like a fool. Flitting around and pretending to be a prying woman from the Harper's Bend book? I even thought of a plot for blackmail based off of how Laurieann Schmitz was behaving. Who can blame someone for thinking the same?"

Charles let his gaze move over Georgette, noting when she immediately set aside the soup that Eunice brought. The way Georgette played with the toast rather than eating it. The way her gaze didn't quite meet anyone else's, and he bit back a groan. "You feel responsible."

"How can I not?"

Marian leapt to her feet and crossed to Georgette, pushing aside the three dogs watching her every move to take her hands. "If I had written Harper's Bend, you wouldn't blame me if some foolish woman decided to act like a character in my book. What if, instead of pretending to be Caroline Hardport, Miss Schmitz had decided to be Iago or Professor Moriarty or Mr. Hyde? You wouldn't blame Shakespeare for Miss Schmitz's foolishness."

Georgette smiled down at Marian and kissed her friend on the forehead. "What did I do to deserve a friend like you?"

"Be the only woman who doesn't bore me to death," Marian shot back with a grin. She pushed to her feet. "Eat your toast, woman. We all feel wan just looking at you."

Obediently, Georgette took a bite of the toast and then repeated, "What did she have?"

"The most horrible journal. I both felt sorry for her and wanted to shake her for some of the things she wrote. She never once talked about blackmail. She wrote if Mr. Thornton knew the truth about Jasper that he'd be disowned forever. She wrote that if Mrs. Yancey wanted to hide the truth of the teashop, she needed to be cleverer. Miss Schmitz is—was—is it is still?"

Georgette nodded. "Her breathing is labored and she's clearly in pain, but she's also unaware of what is happening. A small mercy, I've decided. Ruth was convinced that Laurieann didn't blackmail anyone. Her argument is compelling."

"Then what is happening?" Joseph demanded. He thrust his hands through his hair and groaned. "I don't understand how small-town people think. It's like I'm trying to put together a puzzle and half the pieces are missing."

Georgette sighed and rose to take the afghan from the back of the Chesterfield. She wrapped it around her shoulders. "I spent the day thinking about it. We don't know when the blackmailing started, but it can't have been that long ago if the murderer thought that Miss Schmitz was the blackmailer."

"I suppose that's true." Joseph glanced at Charles and then at Marian before turning back to Georgette.

"So, what if Miss Schmitz began blundering about and someone used that as an opportunity to act on blackmailing?"

"Even if they didn't," Charles said, stretching his neck, "Miss Schmitz was likely confused as the blackmailer by one of the victims, which means—"

"That one of the people she was bothering was also being blackmailed." Georgette took another bite of her toast and then set the plate aside for the mug.

"Which means we can focus on Mrs. Yancey, Mrs. Hanover, Jasper Thornton, Virginia Baker, Miss Hallowton, and you, Georgette," Joseph told her.

Georgette chuckled. "I suppose if it was me, I have been very, very nefarious."

"Why don't we bypass joking about the criminal being Georgette and focus on the other names," Charles said. "What are they hiding?"

Marian shook her head and Joseph groaned. "She never wrote the things down. In case her journal was discovered. There was a fair amount of musing what your secret was, Georgette."

Georgette shivered. Charles took in the sight and rose to get Eunice. "She's got a chill, Eunice. Perhaps some tea?"

Eunice had been sitting in a rocking chair in the kitchen, but she stood and started a tea tray while Charles returned to the parlor only to hear, "I feel bad for Ruth. I would like to help her somehow."

"Of course you do," Marian said. "We'll figure it out together."

Together was the plan. Charles and Joseph just needed these women to let them join the club. Or, Charles thought, the family.

16

GEORGETTE DOROTHY MARSH

Georgette woke the next morning with a gasp and a certainty that her tea had been poisoned. Her back and legs were cramping, and it took her far too long to realize she'd just slept wrapped around her three dogs and pushed to the side. She slowly sat up and stretched her hands towards her feet. Her back ached with a sharp pain while she did, but she waited until her muscles relaxed and the pain started to fade.

"Bea," Georgette told the dog who was licking her cheek, "I blame you."

Bea huffed into Georgette's face.

She decided to make her way to her bath and take a long soak with some salts. Her head was hurting too, and Georgette hoped the reason was because she'd slept poorly and not because she was getting ill.

Georgette started the bath water, turning the hot water

on full blast. She dumped in the salts and then added lavender oil. With the bath near full, Georgette slipped into the water. She'd heard Joseph say he was going to try to track who bought the chocolates and when. If they could identify when the box had been purchased, perhaps they'd be able to identify who had been where at the time. Georgette wanted to know that Ruth would be safe.

Perhaps Georgette wasn't directly responsible for what had happened to Laurieann Schmitz or responsible at all, but she still wanted to know that she'd helped catch her killer. She soaked until the remnants of her dreams had faded and the feeling that she was dying was gone.

Georgette left the bath and dressed in a comfortable wool skirt and jumper with her coziest stockings. She snuggled into her jumper as she went downstairs and found Eunice in the kitchen. The dogs were watching Eunice's every move as she fried bacon and eggs, and Georgette's stomach rolled at the sight of those eggs.

"Hello, darling," Georgette said, pressing her hand to her stomach.

"Miss Georgie," Eunice said as she glanced at her. "You need to add fixing your bed to the list of things to do. I heard you tossing all night long."

"It does squeak, doesn't it?" Georgette took a piece of toast and poured herself a cup of tea before sitting down in the kitchen with Eunice.

"Perhaps I'll just sell it and then buy a new one when we move."

"When?" Eunice asked, surprised, turning from the stove.

"Would you be terribly upset? When I was sitting with Ruth I was just thinking about Laurieann and how she came to Bard's Crook and created for herself a new life. I could do that. We could do it."

"Better than she did, I hope," Eunice said dryly. "I'm prepared to leave Bard's Crook. Miss Georgie, I would like to see you appreciated for your many good qualities. That will never happen here, I fear. Even if you were to break out of how they view you, the moment they realize you wrote those books, you'll be despised."

Georgette tucked her chin onto her palm and stirred her tea. It was the lavender Earl Grey and she adored it. With too much cream and too much sugar, it was a bit like a flowery dessert. She ignored the toast for a shortbread biscuit, dipping it in her tea and popping it into her mouth.

"After all this is over," Georgette said, "I think we should visit a few villages and see if we can find one we like."

Eunice paused, glancing at Georgette, but whatever thought had struck her was not revealed. Georgette finished her tea, thinking she needed to escape the house before Charles tracked her down. He was acting a bit too protective lately, and Georgette intended to do some interfering.

She kissed Eunice on the cheek and left the dogs to their loud objections. She hurried down the back path through the wood to avoid a possible run-in with Charles. When she exited the wood near Mrs. Yancey's teashop, she went around the back of the shop and knocked on the door.

Mrs. Yancey herself opened it. They stared at each other for a moment before she spoke. "I suppose I should be grateful you came to the back."

Georgette stepped away as Mrs. Yancey came out and

closed the door behind her. In silent agreement, they returned to the front of the building to walk down the lane.

"You're being blackmailed," Georgette said.

"Yes," Mrs. Yancey replied.

"Miss Schmitz, the foolish woman, was not the blackmailer."

Mrs. Yancey jerked her gaze from the ground to Georgette's face. "What do you mean?"

"I mean," Georgette replied, "that another person is the blackmailer, and the person who will ultimately be responsible for Miss Schmitz's death is someone who was being blackmailed."

Mrs. Yancey gasped, holding her chest.

Georgette took a deep breath. "Is your secret worth killing for?"

"Why would I tell you, Georgette Marsh? I watched you on occasion when you were a baby. You have no right to my secrets."

Georgette paused as she searched for an answer. "We are, all of us, lonely women—Miss Schmitz. You're a widow. I'm an old-maid. We are all struggling. If we don't stand up for each other and protect one another, who will?"

Mrs. Yancey shook her head, mouth pressed tightly together.

"Come Mrs. Yancey, I have no interest in your secrets."

"She wasn't poisoned in my shop. My girls wouldn't have done it, and I certainly didn't." She stiffened, staring Georgette down. "My secret is mine. I won't reveal it."

Georgette realized she'd get nowhere if Mrs. Yancey continued on as she was. "Your son is in jail, isn't he?" Georgette said. "For stealing from Mr. Thornton, who gave you the money to start your teashop when he realized your son also stole your money."

Mrs. Yancey's lip trembled and she glanced to the side. "My girls—"

Georgette reached out and squeezed Mrs. Yancey's hand. "It's hard, I imagine, to be a mother and feel the need to protect your child at all costs. Not at that cost, though, I don't think."

Mrs. Yancey shook her head. "I might have wanted to strangle Miss Schmitz, but I couldn't risk it. My youngest is only nine, Georgette. No one will care for them if I don't. I would have just tried to soldier through than kill her and risk no one taking care of my girls."

"I doubt that anyone will even seriously consider you. Did you leave your teashop at all yesterday?"

Mrs. Yancey shook her head.

"You have a girl who comes in the morning, don't you?"

"Heather Jones. She was with me in the kitchens."

"You'll need her to just tell Detective Aaron the course of your day. Be very precise and answer his questions honestly. Don't try to sidestep, Mrs. Yancey."

"Mrs. Hanover was being harassed by Miss Schmitz as well. I asked her if she was being blackmailed, and I would swear on my grave that she wasn't, Georgette. Her secret isn't something that you kill over. I can't tell you what it is, but I promise it isn't anything more than embarrassing."

Georgette nodded. "I happen to agree with you. I think I can guess what she's been hiding as well."

Mrs. Yancey stopped, turning Georgette to face her. "How did you know?"

"I suppose I just thought about it," Georgette said. "You went from being rather easy off compared to the rest of us to opening a teashop. It's clear that you're brilliant at it and yet don't love it."

"I don't."

"And, of course, I've met your son and knew that Mr. Thornton had no interest in owning and helping with a teashop, but he paid so much attention to yours. I just—put the pieces together, I suppose."

Mrs. Yancey shook her head and then took Georgette's hand. "How long have you known?"

"Since the beginning."

"You've never said a word."

"I would never."

Mrs. Yancey sniffed and then her bottom lip trembled. "I—"

Georgette saw the apology in Mrs. Yancey's gaze, but Georgette waved it away. She wasn't going to add to Mrs. Yancey's burdens with apologies for things that Mrs. Yancey couldn't have helped.

Instead, Georgette kissed the woman's cheek and left her to hurry to Mrs. Hanover's. When, Mrs. Hanover opened the door she said without greeting, "Miss Schmitz told you, didn't she? I knew she wouldn't keep it quiet. After she had that fake fit the other day, I knew it was coming. I've been hiding out and here you are."

"No one knows," Georgette said, taking Mrs. Hanover's hand. "Well, I know. But no one else knows."

"What do you mean, you know?"

"Mrs. Hanover," Georgette said gently. "I don't think anyone would care that you and Mr. Templeton are seeing each other. I know he's younger than you, but you are a beautiful woman."

Mrs. Hanover's face blushed brilliantly. "We're not! How did you know? Don't tell!"

"I saw you walking with him. He looks at you as though the moon is shining from your eyes. Just marry the man, Mrs. Hanover."

"But, he's ten years younger than I am and rather well off for our times."

"Who cares when he loves you like he does? Don't torture him, Mrs. Hanover. It has been a very long time since you lost your husband. Surely you don't want to be lonely for the rest of your life when a man like Mr. Templeton would make it his personal mission to love and adore you?"

Mrs. Hanover's gaze widened. She reached out to take Georgette's hands. "Do you really think so?"

"I think anyone who does more than lightly tease you about the difference in your ages isn't your friend anyway. Prepare a response for those who would tease you and those who won't let it go. They're the ones you snub from now on."

Mrs. Hanover's eyes lifted. "I suppose you're right."

"If you love him, love him. If you don't, set him free. The man wants to be loved in return, I think."

17

GEORGETTE DOROTHY MARSH

Georgette left Mrs. Hanover, thinking of the remaining names on her list. Miss Hallowton, whose secret Georgette didn't know. Mrs. Baker, who Georgette would just as soon avoid, and Jasper Thornton. She didn't think she had much of a shot with Jasper either. Georgette would have to leave the last two to Joseph Aaron, but Miss Hallowton she could handle.

Georgette walked through the village, stopping at the library. When she entered the building, she saw Miss Hallowton, then she met Charles's gaze. His mouth quirked at her and she wasn't able to hold back her mischievous grin.

"If you're here about the writing group," Mrs. Hallowton told her primly, "it is delayed until Miss Schmitz passes and an appropriate amount of time has elapsed. If you're here about that bedamned book, The Further Adventures of Harper's Bend, I regret to inform you that the waiting list remains full."

Charles chuckled, and Miss Hallowton frowned at him. "They might have more copies in your big city libraries, Mr. Aaron, but I can't justify spending the full budget on a book that no one will wish to read once the fervour has passed."

"Oh, I think they'll want it long after that." Charles's grin was too wide, but Georgette wasn't foolish enough to send him the look he deserved.

Instead she took a seat next to Miss Hallowton. "I need your advice on a few things."

"Is it regarding books?" Miss Hallowton demanded.

"Well, I was hoping for a book about villages around London. Places like Bard's Crook but not Bard's Crook."

Miss Hallowton sniffed and then rose, walking to a shelf where she pulled out two books and returned with them. "And what else?"

Georgette requested to borrow them and also to pick up her mail, and Miss Hallowton stepped away from counter.

"Go away!" Georgette hissed to Charles.

"But I wish to witness this," he protested.

"She won't talk with you around. The only reason she hasn't sent you on your way is that she'd rather have you here than muddying up her house."

Charles grinned, rising and leaning down to Georgette. "You aren't getting away from me again."

Georgette lifted her brows at him as he left the library. She felt as though he'd challenged her.

Miss Hallowton returned and placed a parcel in front of Georgette. "You've been buying a lot of tea."

"My distant uncle, who has been helping me lately, has been quite kind when he heard how fond I am of tea."

"That must be nice," Miss Hallowton said in a tone that spoke the opposite.

"It is indeed," Georgette replied happily. She took the parcel and only just prevented herself from sniffing at the leaves through the wrapping. "Miss Hallowton," Georgette said, glancing about and seeing Charles sitting on a bench across the lane. "Miss Schmitz confided some things to me as I helped her."

"I imagine she had quite a burdened conscience," Miss Hallowton snapped. "I understand she is not expected to survive. I suppose it is not true that only the good die too young. Though, Miss Schmitz is, of course, a bit long in the tooth."

"She is not expected to live." Georgette leaned back and waited, hoping that Miss Hallowton would be compelled to fill the silence. It was a battle of wills, with Miss Hallowton fixing her hard-eyed stare to intimidate Georgette into leaving while Georgette refused to meet Miss Hallowton's gaze, instead drawing on the long history of being nearly always silent to wait for the woman to speak. Georgette won.

"If this is about the secret that I have, it was all a misunderstanding."

"Was it?" Georgette said quietly, still refusing to meet Miss Hallowton's gaze and letting the silence become weighty again.

"There is nothing wrong with doing research about traveling. That doesn't mean that I am not fully reliable in my work or expect to take more than my allotted days."

Georgette bit down on the inside of her mouth to prevent a reply.

"My position is not available. I am a librarian. It is our

business to know a little about a variety of things. There was no need for Miss Schmitz to try to take my position."

"Of course there wasn't," Georgette replied. "I understand that some people Miss Schmitz was bothering were being blackmailed."

Miss Hallowton's jaw snapped shut and then she muttered, "As if I could afford to pay blackmail or would. Why would I? To hide that I was doing my job?"

"Of course not," Georgette said. "It was only idle chatter, Miss Hallowton. I'm sure that Bard's Crook will never have a more responsible librarian than you. We are lucky to have such a...conscientious woman in this position."

Miss Hallowton sniffed sharply. "Too true."

Georgette couldn't help the next bit that slid out. "I am surprised really that Mr. Hadley hasn't been able to convince you to turn your attention from this library to him. I have never seen a man more in love than he is with you."

"Poppycock," Miss Hallowton said, with burning cheeks.

"Oh," Georgette replied. "I am certain it is true. But perhaps, if you do not feel the same, it is easier to not see it?" She rose then, leaving the idea in Miss Hallowton's head.

Georgette was, of course, utterly certain that Miss Hallowton had no idea of Mr. Hadley's affections. She thought, however, that Miss Hallowton might be inclined to recognize Mr. Hadley's brilliance to see all that was lovable about the librarian. Georgette grinned at herself in using the same thought process as the great Jane Austen and hoped to see an equally happy ending for Miss Hallowton and Mr. Hadley.

Georgette left out the side door of the library, much to Miss Hallowton's displeasure, but she didn't let it bother her. There was one more errand that occurred to her on which she could not allow Charles to accompany her. She supposed she would have to apologize rather fiercely to him for it, but it must be done.

If, she thought, she were writing what was happening as a story—then, of course, the less interesting Miss Hallowton, Mrs. Yancey, and Mrs. Hanover must be overlooked for the characters who were truly villainous. Jasper Thornton and Virginia Baker certainly seemed to qualify for those roles. Of the two, Georgette preferred that Virginia Baker was the killer. Was it wrong to wish the woman ill because Georgette simply didn't like her?

She hurried down the street, thinking that Mrs. Baker was not going to tell Georgette a thing. Perhaps if Georgette were to try the same thing as she'd tried with Miss Hallowton and pretend that all had already been revealed?

It was worth an attempt. She turned onto the lane where Mrs. Baker lived and found Joseph Aaron leaving the garden.

"It isn't her," he said as Georgette approached.

"What do you mean?"

"You won't reveal what I am about to tell you?"

Georgette shook her head. "Of course I won't."

"We were able to confirm that Mrs. Baker neither left her house in time to deliver the poisoned chocolates nor could she have bought them. She has rather strained finances. Made worse, mind you, by blackmail. I fear I left her weeping. We were able to track the supplier of the chocolates, and they confirmed that a box was purchased recently. However, they know Mrs. Baker. She buys—

bought—from them regularly. They cut her off after she stopped paying the bill."

Georgette recapped all she'd learned, and then Joseph said to her rather wearily, "Where is Charles?"

"I left him at the library," Georgette replied innocently.

"I might believe that wide gaze of yours if I wasn't aware how clever you are and that Charles is worried over you."

"Why?"

"There's a killer on the loose, Georgette. And you're interfering in the investigation."

"I already knew it wasn't the three that I visited."

His look was utterly exasperated as he demanded, "And Mrs. Baker?"

Georgette tried to look apologetic. When that didn't fly, she said, "I wasn't going to eat or drink anything."

"If Mrs. Baker had been the killer, Georgette, you would have been at risk regardless of whether you consumed anything. If poisoning you didn't work, there could have been any number of ways you died, and then I would be dealing with two murders, a heartbroken uncle, a heartbroken love—if she'll ever give me a chance—and my own guilt. Bloody hell, woman, at least drag Charles into danger with you."

Georgette blinked stupidly at Joseph. Had he...had he... said what she thought he had said?

"Don't look so shocked," Joseph said. "Why else would he be here?"

"For peace and quiet," Georgette suggested quietly.

"In Bard's Crook?" Joseph laughed heartily, but it didn't last. "No more of this putting yourself at risk," he commanded sternly.

Georgette paused, biting her lip.

"What the devil are you up to now?"

Georgette gave him wide, weepy eyes, but it seemed that her tricks wouldn't work on him. She scowled and he only grinned in reply. "There is no scenario, my dear Georgette, where I risk the wrath of my uncle for you to get your way."

"I want to talk to Mr. Thornton."

"He's our most likely suspect," Joseph groaned, shoving his hands into his hair. "Absolutely not."

"Not Jasper. By Jove, Joseph, I'm not an idiot. Mr. Thornton. The father."

"The father?" Joseph asked. "I understood he was away."

"He's only just returned. And he's very...inclined to want to solve a female's problems. To step in and take care of things. He's entirely honorable. There is no chance I'd be in danger."

"Then take Charles with you."

Georgette quickly shook her head and Joseph groaned again, shoving his hands back into his hair. "This is the one who met Charles? At the publishing house?"

Georgette nodded. Joseph took Georgette's arm and led her away from Mrs. Baker's house. "You'll go home immediately after? You won't leave your cottage unless one of us is with you? Until the killer is found?"

Georgette considered long enough to have Joseph scowling at her again.

"Charles will need to come every day to walk the dogs with me and Marian."

"Speaking of Marian," Joseph said, "you'll keep her with you too."

Georgette finally agreed simply to get on with the next step.

She was going to have to cry, she thought. Weep on Mr. Thornton's shoulder and manipulate him into knowing what she knew. In her bones, Georgette was certain that the loud, brash, angry, generally ill-natured and cruel Jasper Thornton had poisoned Miss Schmitz. She just needed Mr. Thornton to recognize it as well because she didn't think they'd catch the son all that quickly if the father didn't help.

18

GEORGETTE DOROTHY MARSH

The Thornton house was, possibly, the largest in the village. It was brick with heavy double doors, a large garden, a wrought iron fence, and it had the little touches that screamed wealth. The best of everything. Surely, Mr. Thornton had lost money in the decline of the economy. They all had, but it seemed that if you started out with enough, you were still quite wealthy even if you were less wealthy.

Georgette found Mr. Thornton sitting in his garden with a book on his lap. She approached him politely, making sure to keep herself as demure as possible. She said as quietly as possible while also being loud enough for him to hear her, "Mr. Thornton?"

He snuffled, jerking away from his snooze, and looked up. His bushy eyebrows lifted rather dramatically in surprise. They seemed to shuffle about his face of their own volition as Georgette asked, "May I speak with you?"

"Of course, my dear, of course." He waved her onto the stone bench where he had been half-snoozing. "What can I do for you?"

For some reason, his face seemed rather solemn and down. Was she reading into his expression what she was about to do to him? Perhaps she wasn't all that clever and only as observant as the average person.

"I—" Georgette found she couldn't lift the handkerchief she'd prepared to her eye and pretend to dab away a tear. This was a good man in front of her. She twisted the handkerchief in her lap, gaze fixed on her hands. "I fear that I need to speak with you about something you'd prefer I didn't."

Mr. Thornton cleared his throat. "You don't need to coddle me, my dear."

Georgette met his gaze and once again, she felt as though he already knew what she was about to say. Was it possible? There looked to be a melancholy knowing in that gaze, or perhaps she was, once again, seeing what she felt should be there.

"I attended Miss Schmitz while the poison was hitting her. I helped to find her cousin, Mrs. Dogger."

Mr. Thornton nodded. His face was white, and Georgette was suddenly sure that he did have an idea of what this was about.

"May I be rudely straightforward with you, Mr. Thornton?"

He nodded again, looking ill.

"Miss Schmitz was acting like a character from the Harper's Bend book because she wanted to be something other than what she was. In the process of it, she listened at doors and ferreted out secrets and tormented people about those things. It was wrong."

Mr. Thornton met Georgette's gaze, and she saw that deep sadness once again.

"But she wasn't an evil woman."

"No," Mr. Thornton agreed. "Laurieann is a good woman."

"And yet," Georgette said, "because someone is blackmailing people from Bard's Crook with secrets they'd prefer to hide and Miss Schmitz was behaving foolishly, she was mistaken as the blackmailer and murdered because of it."

Again, there was no surprise in that gaze.

Georgette reached out and took Mr. Thornton's hand. "Miss Schmitz knew a secret about your son."

"I know," Mr. Thornton said. "I know she did. I talked to her. She said her conscience could not allow her to keep silent."

Georgette leaned back and bit her lip as she realized they both knew what had happened. They were both entirely aware of the murder and who had committed it. She needed, however, Mr. Thornton to help them solve it as quickly as possible.

"She worked for the library on one of the days that Miss Hallowton took off and Miss Schmitz read some of the mail, including a letter from a one-time paramour of my son who needed money for their child."

Georgette gasped, holding her mouth.

"Miss Schmitz rightly guessed that I wouldn't let my grandchild go hungry simply because she was illegitimate and that Jasper was hiding the child's existence from me to avoid being removed from my will."

Georgette pressed her hand harder to her mouth to hold back another gasp and stared with wide, shocked eyes on the man.

Mr. Thornton cleared his throat, avoiding Georgette's gaze. "It's my fault she is dying. I didn't confront Jasper. I left Bard's Crook and went to meet my grandchild. I saw my own eyes staring back at me in that little girl's face. Then I went and visited my nephews. I wanted to see if they, at least, were what they were supposed to be. They are, you know, they're good men. Working hard. Doing right by their families."

Georgette had no idea what to do or say, so she held her silence to keep herself from saying the wrong thing.

"Why are my sons villains and my brother's sons so good? How did I ruin my boys? All that can be said of Heathcliff is that he isn't a murderer. I can't recommend him to the world, Georgette, and he's my own boy."

"It has been repeated to me rather a lot lately that we are not responsible for the choices of others. You were present, Mr. Thornton. You set a good example. You were involved in their lives. I don't know what else you could have done, but I am certain that their choices are not your fault, and I am also certain that your daughter is a good woman."

Mr. Thornton laughed bitterly. "I always neglected her, you know, for my boys. I am a foolish and blind man and too old now to do anything more than regret my life."

Georgette took his hand again. "No! You are a man mourning for his children and the choices they made. You have a daughter who loves you and a granddaughter who, I am sure, wants to love you and time enough to make up for what has passed. Don't let what happened ruin you."

"My son killed that poor woman to hide his crimes from me for money."

Georgette took in a shuddering breath. "Are you certain?"

Thornton nodded, that sick expression back again. "I haven't done anything yet. But I'll have to turn him in, won't I? Laurieann is not dead yet, but she's as good as. She saved little Cordelia and she ruined Jasper."

Georgette shook his hand hard and hissed, "Jasper ruined himself." She paused. "How do you know he did it?"

"It wasn't hard to discover. I talked to Wilkes and found out the details, and then I backtracked knowing it was Jasper. He took the chocolates Nancy bought her mother. He took the strychnine I kept in the cellar for the rats. Easy enough if you're a devil. Maybe if I had been here instead of researching my nephews, I'd have known. I'd have been able to stop him."

Georgette closed her eyes to block the pain on Mr. Thornton's face.

"Do you know what the worst of it is? I wouldn't have objected to him marrying Cordelia's mother. My own wife was a former factory worker. I'm not so old-fashioned that I would turn away a pretty farmer's daughter. Jasper did so because she was nothing to him. Just like the baby was nothing to him. None of this had to happen if Jasper weren't a snobbish, spoiled malcontent who thinks himself better than he is. He's just the child of a man who was lucky and a woman who once was as poor as could be. There is nothing important about us."

Georgette didn't know what to say, so she just held Mr. Thornton's hand, eventually handing over her own handkerchief as he wept silent tears. They sat long enough that

Joseph eventually appeared at the gate. He waited in silence while Georgette rubbed Mr. Thornton's back and then when Mr. Thornton finally noticed Joseph, Georgette whispered she'd take care of the rest.

Georgette walked Mr. Thornton to the door and regretted bitterly her portrayal of him in her book. If only, she thought, she could go back and just write pure fiction. If only she could have trusted herself and not set off this domino of tragedy.

CHARLES AARON

He could tell by the look on her face that she was sick at heart. Gone was the snapping skirt and the clenching and unclenching fists. Instead she walked slowly, as though her body were heavy, and when she reached him she asked, "Do you know what I thought?"

He shook his head, taking her hand and placing it on his arm.

"I thought, if this were a book, I would make Jasper the villain. Rude. Mean, really. Always a bit worse than you'd have imagined. He got sent down from school and no one ever found out why. He doesn't work. Manipulates his mother and is cruel to his sister. There, I thought, of all the people is the villain."

Charles walked Georgette into her own garden and sat with her on the chairs near the willow tree at the back.

"I didn't think about his father, about everyone who would be ruined by his actions. I just watched a man I know to be kind weep into my handkerchief because his son is in fact a villain. I watched him hand over the evidence to arrest his firstborn because it was honorable, and then I held his wife as she cried."

"Georgette," Charles said gently.

"It's not even my fault. Laurieann read the mail when she worked for Miss Hallowton at the library. I didn't have anything to do with that. Or with Laurieann's determination to ensure that the grandfather knew of his grandchild. Or of the fact that anyone who had met Mr. Thornton would know that he would disown his son for abandoning a woman after taking her virtue."

Charles lifted her hand and pressed a kiss on the palm. Her sad, honey brown eyes fixated on his face, and he said, "You're right. None of this is your fault, but you can take credit for being the one to hold both of those parents while they cried, and you can take credit for helping Mr. Thornton give the evidence to convict his son that he was —I am certain—tortured over giving."

Georgette slipped her fingers through Charles's and let him hold her hand. It was the first time that Charles thought she might realize why he was here and utterly the wrong moment to speak what was on his mind. They sat outside until Charles realized Georgette was shivering. He stood, lifting her into his arms, and carried her inside. He took her to Eunice, who met his gaze with lifted brows.

"I fear she is making herself ill."

Eunice's lips twitched but it didn't lessen Charles's worry. Instead he carried Georgette to the Chesterfield in her parlor, covered her with a blanket, lit the fire, and told Eunice, "It wouldn't be a bad thing, I think, to give her some tea with laudanum or a sleeping pill."

Eunice took a sleeping pill from a bottle in the cabinet and carried it to Georgette.

"You need to rest, Miss Georgie."

Rather obediently, Georgette took the pill and curled onto her side. She was, he thought, far, far too good for both Bard's Crook and him. It took her only minutes to fall asleep, and he certainly didn't miss the few tears that made their way down her cheek.

"Out with you," Eunice ordered.

"May I return?"

"I'll be very upset if you don't," Eunice said as Bea leapt onto the sofa and curled up next to Georgette's head and the other two struggled for space at Georgette's feet. "Go on now."

19

If the goddess Atë had turned her wily gaze on Bard's Crook often over the previous days, no one would have been startled. Only the most minxish of creatures would have been interested to see Miss Schmitz slide from sleep into her final rest. Or would want to watch as Mrs. Dogger inherited all that was left of Miss Schmitz's meager fortune and received a very generous donation to start again in another village. Mr. Thornton purchased the little cottage himself to see Mrs. Dogger on her way and then paid for the help in moving her just to ease her passing out of his day-to-day life.

It wasn't those actions that gathered Atë's heart. Neither was it to see the good Scotland Yard detective throw himself at Marian Parker's feet and beg for her love. A romantic goddess, Aphrodite, perhaps, or Guinevere or Psyche might have been interested in that story, but not Atë. Not even when Marian Parker dropped to her knees and cried into the detective's chest a series of yeses, recriminations about not finding her in London, and demands to actually and truly love her.

No, no—what intrigued Atë was when the established and comfortable bachelor walked up the little path to the little stone cottage and found his love, just recovered from her cold, sitting in the garden. Atë gazed with utter hope on the couple as Charles said, "Georgette, surely you know that I love you? That I have come back to Bard's Crook to beg your affections, to plea with you to lay your burdens at my feet, and to wish for your hand?"

Georgette stared at Charles in shock. "I had no such idea."

"How can that be so?"

Georgette took in a deep breath. "Charles, no one has ever loved me or wanted me, not like you're claiming to do. How can I believe this...this...nonsense?"

"Because no one else has had the wit, does that mean it is not possible for me to love you?"

"It means that I am flummoxed," Georgette admitted with an averted gaze. "I don't know how to feel or what to think, and I am certain that I have been living in a fog only to escape into this surreal haze of just beginning to create my own fate. I barely am comfortable with being happy with what I have to expect more. I don't even know what I want for the future. I keep expecting my present happiness to burn away."

Charles took her hand. "So you don't want me?"

Georgette glanced at him, her baffled feelings clear. "Don't you see? You're Mr. Darcy. You're handsome and kind and clever and you helped me to save myself, and I feel as though I am Charlotte Lucas and you're seeing Elizabeth Bennett. I am not Lizzie, Charles. I am certain you will only be disappointed in me, and then we'll both knock about in misery, regretting this moment forever. I can't do that."

Charles laughed. "I am no Mr. Darcy."

"I find you occupy the same place in my mind as Mr. Darcy, Charles, and I can't imagine that we would fit."

"What do I have to do to convince you?" he asked, shocked to find himself being turned down.

"I need to believe," she told him honestly, "in my heart of hearts that you see all of my Charlotte Lucas-ness and you want me all the same." She paused, and she tried to find the words for the rest.

Charles seemed to understand her because he waited for her to finish.

"And," Georgette said quietly. "I have to believe that we will be happier together than we are apart. I only just found happiness and peace with my life, Charles. I'm afraid to rock my own boat and find myself capsized."

He cupped her cheek and leaned forward, leaving a kiss on her forehead. "You know, neither of us are characters in a book, but if you need time to believe that I love you and will continue to love you, I will give you that time."

She dabbed a tear away from the edge of her eye, terrified she'd ruined all the chances she would ever have at love. She stared at him, uncertain of what to say, but found that gentle smile and warm gaze fixed on her face as though she weren't a plain old-maid.

"We're going to have raucous fights one day, love," he told her, "but you'll always know that I love you when we do. We're going to have children one day and look at them in awe at times and in horror at others. We'll share a house, and we won't have a happily ever after, because that is a fairy tale and this will be our real life. Not an ending that ends with a kiss, but with two wrinkled, old husks who hold hands in the sun, grateful for all the days we had together and jealous that we can't have even more."

Georgette stared at Charles as he slowly leaned in and kissed her on the lips. It was her very first kiss and the very first time she thought he might be in earnest.

"I have to go back to London," he told her. "Don't get comfortable without me, as I'll be back."

Georgette stared in shock as he left, and the goddess Atë cackled in utter delight.

The END

Hullo, my friends, I have so much gratitude for you reading my books. Almost as wonderful as giving me a chance are reviews, and indie folks, like myself, need them desperately! If you wouldn't mind, I would be so grateful for a review.

THE SEQUEL TO THIS BOOK IS AVAILABLE NOW.

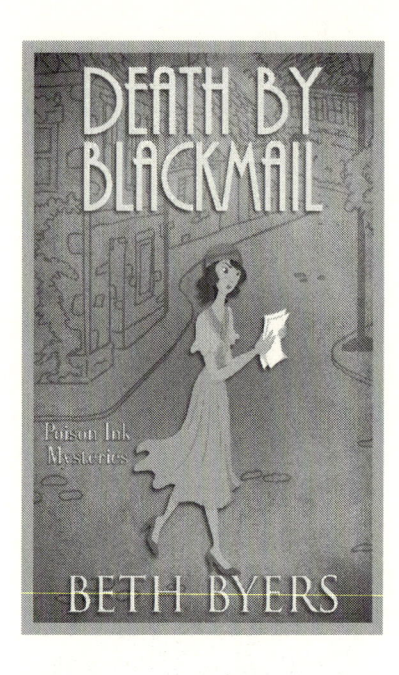

When Georgette watches a neighbor murdered over her book, she thinks the world has gone mad. With her second book on the market and mostly fiction, she expects things to go back to normal. Only another person dies. The deaths clarify her path needs to be one that leaves her hometown, Harper's Bend, behind.

A decision that is further elucidated when she receives a blackmail letter. As Georgette deliberates what to do, she turns to her friend, Charles Aaron. Before she has even completed her explanation, another body falls. Has the blackmailer decided to ruin his victims by killing them instead of taking all their money? If so, is Georgette at risk? And will Georgette and her friends find the killer before all of her secrets out?

Order your copy here.

If you want book updates, you could follow me on Facebook.

ALSO BY BETH BYERS

THE VIOLET CARLYLE COZY HISTORICAL MYSTERIES

Murder & the Heir

Murder at Kennington House

Murder at the Folly

A Merry Little Murder

New Year's Madness: A Short Story Anthology

Valentine's Madness: A Short Story Anthology

Murder Among the Roses

Murder in the Shallows

Gin & Murder

Obsidian Murder

Murder at the Ladies Club

Weddings Vows & Murder

A Jazzy Little Murder

Murder by Chocolate

A Friendly Little Murder

Murder by the Sea

Murder On All Hallows

Murder in the Shadows

A Jolly Little Murder

Christmas Madness: A Short Story Anthology

Hijinks & Murder

Love & Murder

A Zestful Little Murder (coming soon)

A Murder Most Odd (coming soon)

Nearly A Murder (coming soon)

THE POISON INK MYSTERIES

Death By the Book

Death Witnessed

Death by Blackmail

Death Misconstrued

Deathly Ever After

Death in the Mirror

A Merry Little Death

Death Between the Pages

THE 2ND CHANCE DINER MYSTERIES

(This series is complete.)

Spaghetti, Meatballs, & Murder

Cookies & Catastrophe

Poison & Pie

Double Mocha Murder

Cinnamon Rolls & Cyanide

Tea & Temptation

Donuts & Danger

Scones & Scandal

Lemonade & Loathing

Wedding Cake & Woe

Honeymoons & Honeydew

The Pumpkin Problem

THE HETTIE & RO ADVENTURES

cowritten with Bettie Jane

(This series is complete.)

Philanderer Gone

Adventurer Gone

Holiday Gone

Aeronaut Gone

ALSO BY AMANDA A. ALLEN

THE MYSTIC COVE MOMMY MYSTERIES

Bedtimes & Broomsticks

Runes & Roller Skates

Banshees and Babysitters

Hobgoblins and Homework

Christmas and Curses

Valentines & Valkyries

THE RUE HALLOW MYSTERIES

Hallow Graves

Hungry Graves

Lonely Graves

Sisters and Graves

Yule Graves

Fated Graves

Ruby Graves

THE INEPT WITCHES MYSTERIES

(co-written with Auburn Seal)

(This series is complete.)

Inconvenient Murder

Moonlight Murder

Bewitched Murder

Presidium Vignettes (with Rue Hallow)

Prague Murder

Paris Murder

Murder By Degrees

Copyright © 2019 by Beth Byers, Amanda A. Allen

All rights reserved.

No part of this book may be reproduced in any form or by any electronic or mechanical means, including information storage and retrieval systems, without written permission from the author, except for the use of brief quotations in a book review.

❀ Created with Vellum

Made in the USA
Las Vegas, NV
20 April 2024